"I don't know much about ranching."

"You can learn."

Nathan was hoping she'd say that because it was exactly what he planned to do. *Had* to do. "Are you available?"

Her profile hardened.

"I didn't mean it that way." He held up both hands. "Look, maybe we got off on the wrong foot."

"Maybe we didn't."

He huffed a frustrated sigh and tried again. "Name's Nathan Garrison." He offered a handshake. She didn't take it. "Persimmon Hill is my property and I plan to revive it as a guest ranch."

"Must be nice to be that rich."

He wasn't, and he stood to lose more than he could afford, including this property. "You know my name. Aren't you going to tell me yours?"

She looked him over as if deciding if he was worthy of the honor. "Monroe Matheson," she said, then faced the aging mansion. "And I have one request. Make Persimmon Hill shine again and erase that one tragedy from everyone's memory."

Erase the tragedy? How he wished he could.

Linda Goodnight, a *New York Times* bestselling author and winner of a RITA® Award in Inspirational Fiction, has appeared on the Christian bestseller list. Her novels have been translated into more than a dozen languages. Active in orphan ministry, Linda enjoys writing fiction that carries a message of hope in a sometimes-dark world. She and her husband live in Oklahoma. Visit her website, lindagoodnight.com, for more information.

Books by Linda Goodnight

Love Inspired

Sundown Valley

The Buchanons

Love Inspired Trade

Visit the Author Profile page at LoveInspired.com for more titles.

The Rancher's Sanctuary

Linda Goodnight

LOVE INSPIRED
INSPIRATIONAL ROMANCE

LOVE INSPIRED®
INSPIRATIONAL ROMANCE

Recycling programs
for this product may
not exist in your area.

ISBN-13: 978-1-335-58646-9

The Rancher's Sanctuary

Copyright © 2023 by Linda Goodnight

For questions and comments about the quality of this book, please contact us at CustomerService@Harlequin.com.

Love Inspired
22 Adelaide St. West, 41st Floor
Toronto, Ontario M5H 4E3, Canada
www.LoveInspired.com

Printed in U.S.A.

He shall cover thee with his feathers,
and under his wings shalt thou trust.
—*Psalm* 91:4

As always, to bring glory to the Father, Son and Holy Spirit and with loving gratitude for the gift of story.

Chapter One

What happened in that house?

Nathan Garrison stopped his blue F-150 Ford truck at the end of a long, curving driveway shrouded in brush and overgrown trees. Twenty-four years had passed since he'd last seen this once-glorious property on the outskirts of Sundown Valley, Oklahoma. Twenty-four years and a lifetime of questions.

He'd never expected to see his childhood home again, didn't know it still existed until last week, but now Persimmon Hill was his.

If he could keep it.

So many lies and half-truths surrounded his childhood and this property that he was determined to unravel the tangled weeds and find answers.

Six months was a short amount of time, but that's all he had.

If he didn't succeed, he'd lose more than money, he'd lose the final piece of himself.

He could not live the rest of his life with this emptiness inside him.

From this half-mile distance, Nathan couldn't see the house, but newspaper clippings displayed a property of significant beauty. The sprawling guest ranch on Persimmon Hill now belonged to him. His father's dream. The house where both his parents had died.

Twenty-four years later, he still didn't understand why.

With a slow, steadying inhale, he filled his lungs with southern Oklahoma's clean, rural air, the first he'd breathed since being whisked away from here when he was barely old enough to comprehend what he'd seen and heard.

Today, the images were as vivid as they'd been that morning when he, at age six, had trotted down the stairs stretching and yawning, innocently unaware that his life was about to change forever.

After stepping out of the truck, Nathan unlocked the wide gate and swung it inward toward the property. A basic iron structure that he might see on any number of nearby ranches, this gate was different from the fancy wrought-iron double estate gate that had once proclaimed the letter *V* to passersby. V for Vandiver, his father's name, a name no longer his. Another mystery. Another half-truth.

A faded no-trespassing notice tied with rusted baling wire rattled against the silver gate. He had no idea who'd put it there or when.

Tattered and barely readable, a Realtor's sign leaned half-hidden against a stately brick column that had once served as one end of a pair that bracketed the estate gate. The long grass around the bricks waved in the soft breeze as if whispering secret warnings.

Go back. Go back. You don't really want to know.

He couldn't. He was in too deep, both emotionally and financially. Turning back was no longer an option.

In defiance of his imagination, Nathan jerked the sign from the ground, scattering moist earth and roots before tossing it in the bed of the truck.

Some go-getter real estate agent could forget it. Persimmon Hill had never been for sale.

He hadn't known that, of course, until now. His grandparents had led him to believe Persimmon Hill was sold long ago.

When the attorney's phone call had come on his thirtieth birthday, he'd been shocked to learn that not only was Persimmon Hill intact but that the guest ranch now belonged to him.

When he'd demanded answers from his grandparents, Grandmother had burst into tears.

Grandpa told him to sell out and forget Persimmon Hill ever existed.

"For your own good," they'd claimed.

That was the way it had always been.

Anytime he'd asked about his parents or the home he remembered, Grandmother cried and Grandpa drank.

He knew what his father was accused of doing. So, why the secrecy? Was it shame? Were they afraid the stigma would destroy him? Or were they hiding something more sinister?

What could be more sinister than what he'd seen that morning when he was six years old?

And why could he never shake the feeling that he remembered something that he could not quite bring to the fore?

Nevertheless, he'd learned to remain silent, keeping the questions and fears to himself. He'd been a quiet child, tiptoeing through his grandparents' broken hearts.

But everything was different now. He was a man and, though he never wanted to hurt his loving grandparents, he'd never be completely at peace until he found answers.

The memories of his childhood were locked away inside him and inside Persimmon Hill. The only photo of his parents he owned was from an old newspaper he'd discovered as a teenager.

And always, always he carried a vague, gut-deep knowing that made a lie of the official police report.

Leaning his forearms atop the pickup bed rails, he gazed out over the quiet Kiamichi countryside.

Maybe it was jitters, nerves, whatever. Maybe he feared failure. No *maybe* about it, for suddenly Nathan was in no hurry to drive around the curves and go beyond the thick trees.

He knew little about ranching. Nothing about investigating a long-ago crime.

One thing for certain, his past was a muddy, bloody river he'd needed to swim for so long he wasn't sure what part was imagination and which was real.

His entire future and much of his past was riding on the next six months.

A prickle of sweat beaded on his neck that had nothing to do with the sun, already high in a sky as blue as his mother's eyes.

Beneath the cotton-ball clouds, a red-tailed hawk circled, a predator ever on the hunt. As the winged shadow passed, a covey of ground birds scattered into the underbrush.

As if in defiance of the predatory hunter, a roadrunner zigzagged in madcap fashion along the grassy edge of a barbed wire fence.

The zany, comical bird with his straight back and head high reminded Nathan of a cartoon he'd loved as a kid. Still watched sometimes when he wanted to laugh and remember the good times in the house on Persimmon Hill.

While he would lie on his belly watching Saturday morning cartoons, Mother would sit at the table, listening to Dad over coffee and waffles. Though saying little, Mother would lean her chin on upraised knuckles and smile as though Dad was the smartest man on earth. He'd hold her other hand across the table, tender and loving. And they'd both loved him.

Even though memories were vague, he knew deep down in the very core of him that they'd been devoted to each other and to him.

His life had been Camelot.

So what had happened?

Why had his grandparents refused to talk about them? About *it*? Why hadn't they told him that he was heir to his parents' dream guest ranch? Why had they led him to believe Persimmon Hill had long ago been sold?

He didn't know, and he had only a six-month leave of absence and a substantial but short-term loan to juggle everything into place or lose it all.

Sighing, he climbed back inside the truck and started the engine. The rumbling noise seemed out of place in the cemetery-like stillness.

A cottontail rabbit scurried across the driveway in his path. Overhead the red-tailed hawk made his move, diving at breathtaking speed.

Nathan put the truck in Drive, revved the

motor and roared up the overgrown road. The hawk swooped over the hood, missing the hapless bunny and his lunch. There would be no death at Persimmon Hill today.

Fighting morbid thoughts, Nathan eased around the curves and past the brooding over-hang of oaks and sycamores. Their leaves dappled the roadway in shadows and swished against the truck's top and sides as if trying to hold him back.

This part of rural Oklahoma was as remote as it was beautiful. Bad things shouldn't happen here.

And never would again if he had any say in the matter.

When he rounded the last curve and broke into full sunlight, he noticed the house first. Mouth dry, eyes wide and fixated, Nathan scanned the stately two-and-a-half-story structure. Persimmon Hill stared back at him with heavily shuttered, darkened windows like eyes that could not bear to open again.

A rush of emotions clogged Nathan's throat. His whole being seized up, still yearning for the young parents he'd never stopped missing but barely remembered.

If houses could talk. *This* house. Would it tell him what he needed to hear? Or would it only confirm the worst?

Nathan reached for the travel cup at his side and swigged down a gulp of bittersweet emotion. Movement dragged his attention to the sprawling front porch with its glorious white columns reaching two stories like something out of a Grecian painting. A long-legged woman leaned her back against one of the columns, a booted foot resting on the porch, the other trailing the grass. A gaggle of dogs of all sorts and sizes roamed around her, as if vying for her touch.

His first impression was that she was a cowgirl version of a beautiful dream. Miss Cowgirl USA or a rodeo queen. Posture relaxed, maybe a little insolent, she looked up and glared at the interruption to her solitude.

His mind took snapshots.

Covered in snug, faded jeans stuffed into brown cowgirl boots with turquoise accents, her legs were long enough to notice. And Nathan definitely noticed. He was a Christian, but he wasn't dead. God made beauty to appreciate.

This beauty was a Western painting.

A gauzy turquoise blouse of Southwest design fluttered in the gentle breeze of early spring. Thick blond hair swooped over each shoulder and caressed the sides of her face. The hand stroking the head of a small, homely black dog bore a turquoise ring on each of four fingers.

Who was this intriguing stranger and what was she doing here, trespassing on his property?

Monroe Matheson was annoyed. Plain and simple, some rhinestone cowboy in his business suit, cowboy boots, hat and fancy truck had intruded upon her favorite place of solitude. No one was allowed to come here. No one.

At least twice a week, she and her dogs escaped to Persimmon Hill, knowing they would be left alone.

No one had ever disturbed them before. Not even once in all the years she'd used the house on Persimmon Hill as her secret escape.

Then, *he* had to show up. And she didn't even have a weapon.

Stranger danger didn't scare Monroe. She was a military veteran. She could take care of herself. She just wanted him to go away.

The man sauntered across the raggedy, overgrown grass and approached the porch. Monroe braced herself for fight or flight, though she refused to appear ruffled. *Never let 'em see you sweat.* That was her motto. One of several.

"Are you a real cowboy or did you just find the hat?" She sounded as bored and cold as she could manage. Which was considerable. She practiced a lot.

The stranger laughed. Perfect white teeth and stunningly attractive smile lines appeared. Somewhere a choir broke out in a chorus of exaltation.

Handsome was a pale word to describe this one.

He removed the hat, a black Stetson that had set him back at least $500, and rested it against his trouser-clad thigh. A *black* hat to boot, like the bad guys in a movie. But in the sunshine, he was all golden-boy handsome with a smile to break a woman's heart and an easy, confident air. He was a cross between a young Brad Pitt and the hunky guy who played Thor. If he wasn't in movies, he should be.

Anywhere but here on this deserted old ranch where Monroe came to think and, when the mood struck, to pray and be mad at God without censor from her grandpa.

The city slicker—for he must be city in that getup—was confidently beautiful in the way only the most masculine men can be.

Whoever he was, Monroe loathed him on sight.

She kept up her assault, hoping to send him scurrying away like the squirrels that fled up the giant pecan tree whenever she and her pack of once-stray dogs loped into the yard.

"Can't you read?" Keeping her face in profile, she nonchalantly rubbed the ears of Torpedo, the part terrier, mostly mutt with the energy level of a nuclear power plant.

The man replaced the hat, shading silvery-blue eyes. "Sure. Can you?"

She ignored his question. "I don't know where you come from, but out here, no-trespassing signs mean business. You could get yourself shot."

"Houston. You gonna shoot me?"

"Maybe." She didn't laugh. Men, in general,

needed shooting, to her way of thinking. "How did you get that truck through a locked gate? Run it over? Pick the lock?"

He extracted a key from his shirt pocket and held it up. The cone-shaped silver glinted in the sunlight.

Monroe frowned, calculating the meaning of this man, in his big, fancy truck, with a key to the abandoned property on Persimmon Hill. *Her* spot for years, even before leaving for the navy.

"You a Realtor?"

"Why do you ask?"

"You look like one." The kind who wore a cowboy hat and boots for effect, hoping to appear good-old country boy while he charmed people out of their ranchland. The Matheson family had already encountered a creep like that. Only this new guy was far better looking.

"What are you doing here?" She shifted, careful to keep her face averted, and eased the terrier to the porch. He snuggled close to her side, needy like all her strays. "Don't tell me you're buying this place."

The stranger shrugged. An annoying little tilt edged his mouth, as if he found her questions amusing. "Okay, I won't tell you."

Jerk. Typical male. Thinks he's all that and a ticket to the moon.

Letting herself grow angry, which was easy to do anytime an unrelated male came around,

Monroe slung both booted feet to the ground and stood up so fast three dogs tumbled over each other and the ever-trembling Torpedo yelped, insulted but unhurt. The other two rushed in to wrestle and play around her legs, something Monroe was in no mood to do. This man had ruined her tranquility.

Too bad none of her dogs would bite. Even Peabody, the battered and scarred pit bull mix, was a sissy. Silly animals. They accepted anyone and everyone who was nice to them and even those who weren't.

"Didn't the Realtor tell you the story of this place?" she asked. "Warn you away?"

"From what? The property is beautiful. Pretty neglected but the bones are excellent."

Seriously? He didn't know? How could he have purchased an estate of this size without learning its history? Granted, the incident happened years ago and people had long stopped talking about it. The secluded property attracted little attention these days. That's why she liked it.

"Bad things happened here."

Something in his expression shuttered. The quirky smile flattened. "Like what?"

"Murder."

Chapter Two

Nathan winced.

The official story was more complicated, but always ended with that one word. *Murder.*

Nathan had known what she would say, but if he was to discover anything other than this as truth, he needed to let people talk while he, like his late mother, listened. He knew how to do that.

His problem was keeping his quest for information a secret while reopening the guest ranch and quietly probing the population of the nearby small town for memories of his family. They'd had friends. They'd entertained. He vaguely recalled dinner parties in the dining room and barbecues on the large patio. Someone could shed more light on who they were and, perhaps, why they'd died.

Nathan slid his hands into the back pockets of his jeans, hoping for casual while his heart ricocheted off his rib cage and he faced a less-than-friendly female who might know things he didn't.

Around his age, she was beautiful, at least what part of her face he could see, but she clearly had an anger issue. At humans, anyway. She was gentle and sweet with the five dogs circling around her like a canine merry-go-round.

"So what's the story," he prodded, hoping to learn something without revealing too much.

Nathan wasn't ready for folks in Sundown Valley to connect him with the Persimmon Hill of the past. Not until he learned everything he could about Mother and Dad. He wanted the unvarnished truth, not sympathy or gory stories.

Better that they saw him as a developer whose only interest in the guest ranch was monetary. Even that presented problems. Six months was not much time to restore an entire guest ranch that had been sitting empty for nearly a quarter century.

"People say the place is haunted." The cowgirl didn't face him head-on. She stood at an angle, gazing at the house.

"I don't believe in that kind of thing."

"Neither do I." She shrugged those elegant shoulders, sending the gauzy shirt into another flutter in the cool spring air. "Some people around here do. I think that's partly why the place hasn't been ransacked by vandals."

"And the other part?"

"The crime happened a long time ago. The house sits off the road, secluded. People move on and forget."

He hadn't. Regardless of his grandparents' silence, he could never forget.

"What exactly occurred? Was the killer ever caught?" Nathan knew the answers but wanted to hear them from a source other than a couple of old newspapers.

The drumbeat of hopeful tension dried out his throat and made his breathing shallow. He forced himself to appear calm and only mildly interested, at least on the surface.

"Murder-suicide. A man shot his wife and then himself. So yes, I guess you'd say the killer was caught." She kept her face averted, as if she dared not look him in the eye when revealing such an evil.

Nathan had been braced to hear this. During his research, he'd read the lurid account in old newspapers. He knew what his dad was accused of doing, the reason his grandparents hated Paul Vandiver and refused to utter his name. Still, the words spoken aloud sliced him to the bone.

He fought down the need to protest. His father wasn't that kind of man. Yes, Nathan had only been six years old, but he refused to believe this monstrous tale, no matter that the official police ruling was murder-suicide. Could not *let* himself believe such a thing about the father whose blood ran through his own veins.

Dad had been a good man, a Christian. Hadn't he?

Nathan swallowed, stacked a fist on each hip and turned aside for a moment, waiting for his thudding, aching heart to settle into a normal rhythm.

"Not the house's fault," he heard the woman murmur. "It's lonely."

For some reason, the wistful comment from this chilly stranger soothed Nathan a little. Somewhere inside that icy beauty was a kindness she hid from all except her pack of pups. Which made him wonder about her.

He turned back to find her in a crouch, several dogs crowding in for her attention. They were a ragged pack, scarred, or missing a limb or an ear or an eye. She touched each one, murmuring words meant only for the dog, though he heard her praises as she gave out "good boys" and "sweethearts." A thick waterfall of pale blond hair tumbled forward and brushed the dogs while concealing the features he'd barely glimpsed.

Nathan's curiosity about the cowgirl increased. "I agree. Houses don't kill people. It's a beautiful old mansion. There was joy here as well as that one awful tragedy."

She offered him another appraising side-eye.

"Are you going to live here?" The sharp tone had returned to her voice.

"Why do you ask?"

She shrugged and snuggled her face against the pit bull's thick, muscular neck. Numerous disfiguring scars covered the animal's body, especially his face and neck.

"No reason. I just find it odd after so many years that someone would buy the place. Persimmon Hill has been empty for a long time."

Nathan didn't bother saying that he hadn't bought it. No one needed to know that he was the boy who'd discovered his parents that horrible morning. Resurrecting the memories in himself and digging for answers would be hard enough without inducing pity in the people who'd known his parents. He didn't want sympathy. He wanted the truth.

His gaze swept across the broad horizon, taking in trees, ponds and pasture along with the myriad buildings spread across the thousands of acres. Not that he could see them all from here, but the lawyer had given him the rundown. Eight cabins, two other homes, seven barns, six sheds, though he didn't yet know how much of the equipment and furnishings still remained.

Even though the trust money, now gone, had been spent on insurance, taxes and, in the past, some basic upkeep, an empty property invited thieves and decay.

Nathan prayed the place was mostly intact so he could move quickly. If he was forced to sell Persimmon Hill to repay the restoration loan, he'd never find the missing piece of himself.

He could not let that happen.

Nathan turned back to the woman. He still didn't know her name or why she was here. Another mystery.

"I haven't been inside." At least, not as an adult. "Have you?"

Shaking her head, she dispatched the adoring dogs and stood. She wasn't as tall as her long legs suggested but tall enough to look him in the eyes.

Except she didn't. For some odd reason, she kept her head lowered and turned slightly away. Parted on one side, thick pale hair covered the averted portion of her face.

A coy movement of a beautiful woman, perhaps? A ploy to intrigue and attract?

She certainly didn't seem the type. But she was beautiful…and intriguing.

"You never said what you're doing on my property," he coaxed in his most charming voice, unwilling to see her leave, hoping she'd tell him more, even if it was useless gossip about a long-ago tragedy. Or about herself.

"I didn't know it had sold until now."

Which didn't answer his question. Why was she here? Where had she come from? He didn't see a vehicle.

She was a blonde like his late mother. Maybe she was a figment of his imagination, a product of his longing to see his mother one more time.

He shook his head and nearly scoffed. He was not going down the haunted road. His faith was in God, not ghosts, even if he was a captive to his past.

"How did *you* get in here? The gate's chained and padlocked." Though tempted to repeat her accusation of picking the lock, he thought better of it. She didn't seem the type of woman to appreciate his humor.

"My horse."

He jacked an eyebrow. He hadn't noticed any sign of an animal other than the scraggly dogs. "Horse?"

She snorted. "Now I know you found the hat. Yes, greenhorn, a horse. A four-legged creature with a strong back and big, soft eyes. He's around here somewhere, mowing the grass."

Good for the horse. Grass was knee-high. The whole place needed a tractor and brush hog for days on end. "I know what a horse is."

She tossed her head. "Could have fooled me. But if you bought this enormous spread, you either know ranching or you'll have to learn. Unless you're going to raze the buildings and start over." Her tone darkened, grew intense as if she'd personally horsewhip him out of the country if he desecrated the property.

He couldn't help teasing her a little. "What if I want to build a housing addition?"

"Do you?" One perfect eyebrow dipped low. He still couldn't see the other one. "Don't do that."

He pretended to consider the option. "I have to do something with the property, and I don't know much about ranching."

"You can learn."

He was hoping she'd say that because it was exactly what he planned to do. *Had* to do.

"Are you available?"

Her hand froze on the white head of the pit bull. Her profile hardened as cold as an ice pack on a warm back.

"I didn't mean it that way." He held up both hands. "Look, maybe we got off on the wrong foot."

"Maybe we didn't."

He huffed a frustrated sigh and tried again. "Name's Nathan Garrison." He offered a handshake. She didn't take it. "Persimmon Hill is my property and I plan to revive it as a guest ranch."

"Must be nice to be that rich."

He wasn't, and unless he worked quickly, he stood to lose more than he could afford, including this property.

"You know my name. Aren't you going to tell me yours?"

She looked him over as if deciding if he was worthy of the honor. She gathered a scrawny leaf-laden mongrel into her arms and snuggled him against her neck.

"Monroe Matheson," she said, then turned her back and faced the aging mansion. "I'm not one to ask for favors, but I have one request. Make Persimmon Hill shine again. A house this beautiful deserves someone to love it again and to erase that one tragedy from everyone's memory."

Erase the tragedy? How he wished he could.

Nevertheless, her observation surprised him. She'd been nothing but rude since his arrival, but she obviously felt strongly about Persimmon Hill.

So did he, for reasons she wouldn't understand. Or maybe she would. He didn't know her yet.

The *yet* hung up in his brain. He had plenty of complications in his life right now. Did he really want to add a snarky, difficult cowgirl to the growing list?

"Why do you care?" he asked.

"Didn't say I did." She pivoted slightly to look at him.

"But you do."

"Yes." Her voice went soft and low as if the admission was hard for her. The chip on her shoulder was a boulder she could barely see around. "My family ranches a much smaller spread. When the big ones like Persimmon Hill disappear, we'll all be the worse for it."

"Were you friends of the previous owners?"

She sniffed, grunted. "Do I look that old? I was a toddler when it happened."

He'd stuck his foot in his mouth again. "I meant, did your family know them? Do you remember them at all? Who they were?"

"Lisa and Paul Vandiver. They were friends of my parents'. I remember that much. Or maybe I heard my parents talk about them at some point. I don't know."

He hadn't been asking their names. He knew those. He wanted to know *them*. Who were Paul and Lisa beyond his vague memories? Why had this happened to them? Why were they dead and he was still alive?

Yet, Nathan's hope rose. The cynical Monroe had given him his first contact. Her parents. If they knew Lisa and Paul, they also might know if there were marital or financial problems or, better yet, give him a glowing report of the kind of loving relationship he *thought* he remembered.

"Well, Monroe." He liked the name. It fit her. A tough cowgirl with a touch of movie-star mystique and a whole lot of spit-in-your-eye. "Maybe you could give me a tour of the place."

"Why would I do that? Didn't you look at it before you bought it? Or are you one of those rich people who buy investment properties sight unseen from the internet?"

Difficult woman. Where he came from, people were friendly to strangers. In fact, the nearby town had been as friendly as this passel of tail-wagging canines now vying for his attention. But not her.

"Being neighborly? Southern hospitality?"

She seemed to contemplate the idea of walking around the property with him in the same way she'd contemplate the decision to pick up a rattlesnake.

Why had she taken an instant dislike to him? Was it because he'd encroached on her solitude? Or was she rude to everyone? What had caused that chip on her shoulder?

Inwardly, he scoffed at the flood of questions. No doubt about it, the cowgirl intrigued him.

A squatty, pug-nosed creature as wide and low to the ground as a small car sniffed around Nathan's pant legs, its clogged-sinus breathing loud.

Another, this one as fluffy and golden as his grandma's cocker spaniel but three times bigger, parked its behind on Nathan's shoe. A setter, he thought, with humor. The dog looked up at him with only one eye. The other eye was permanently closed.

Going to his haunches, Nathan was instantly inundated with furballs. Laughing, he braced a hand behind him to keep from being bowled over.

"I think they like me."

"Animals are dumb like that."

Coming to expect the sarcasm, he actually managed a grin. "So, are you and these dumb animals going to show me around?"

With a beleaguered sigh, she looked up at the sky and shook her head as if he was as dumb as her dogs. "If I do, will you leave?"

He laughed again. "Can't. I'm moving in."

Monroe figured that was the worst news she'd heard all day. While she was glad this man, Nathan Garrison, wouldn't bulldoze the mansion and build a row of cookie-cutter houses, he made her itchy. She knew too well the results of that itchy feeling in her chest. Some women called it attraction. Monroe called it trouble. She wanted to rip the feeling right out of her and stomp it into silence.

Once Mr. Charming-and-Way-Too-Handsome Nathan got a good look at her, he wouldn't want her to walk the property with him. He'd want to throw up.

So far, she'd managed to avoid the inevitable expressions of horror followed by pity that were then followed by averted eyes and a quick departure.

She wanted to get away before that happened.

So why didn't she just leave?

"Sorry," she said. "Can't stay. You're on your own."

Taking one of the smaller dogs into his arms, the rhinestone cowboy stood up. Rake, a scraggly mass of tangled fur with a missing paw, licked the man's face. Traitor. After all the kibble and medicine she'd pumped into his cute, wounded body, Rake now abandoned her for the handsome, pseudo-cowboy who'd bought a ranch but admitted knowing nothing about ranching.

Who did that?

Rich boys with nothing else to do. *Pretty* rich boys.

"Your dog likes me," Nathan said. "Doesn't that tell you something?"

"Yes. It tells me you probably smell like whatever fast food you had for lunch."

He laughed and those charming smile creases winked at her. He was good at that. Easy laughter, as if his life had been all rainbows and butterflies. Prince Charming with lots of money and an easy life.

He'd probably never had his heart broken.

In spite of herself, her gaze strayed to his left hand. No ring. Which didn't mean a thing these days.

Married or not, drugstore cowboys weren't her type.

In fact, no one was her type. Not anymore. Not since Tony had taken one look at her face and suddenly decided he didn't want to get married after all.

The bitter pill of betrayal soured her stomach.

No use letting golden cowboy Nathan know she found him attractive. That could be lethal.

"What's his name?" he asked as if she hadn't gone as silent as stone.

"Rake."

Both his eyebrows shot up. "Interesting name."

"But apropos." Sometimes she tossed out a fifty-cent word to remind people that although she might be ugly, she still had a brain. "He tends to gather leaves and twigs in his fur no matter how often I brush him."

"What happened to his paw?"

"Amputated. The whole leg was a mess when I found him and the vet couldn't save the paw."

"He gets around well."

"Dogs are adaptable, if humans give them a chance." She knew she sounded angry. She was. Abandoning a dog on the side of the road ranked right up there with poison pond scum in her book.

"Well, Rake, my friend—" Nathan put his nose close to the tongue-lolling mutt "—want to join my explorations?"

The man was determined, she'd give him that. He'd already figured out she was devoted to her animals and wouldn't leave them.

"Maybe I'll sit on the porch and wait while you two take a stroll."

"Why not go with us? We promise to be good company." He ruffled Rake's messy ears. "Won't we, buddy? Let's check out the house first."

He tossed the last out like a fishing lure. The

man must be a salesman. He'd already figured out that she loved the house.

Monroe felt herself giving in. "I've always wanted to see the interior."

Smiling, Nathan extended the key. "Lead the way."

She narrowed her eyes. If he'd looked the least bit smug at her capitulation, she'd have slapped the key out of his hand. He didn't. Like a man used to waiting, he dangled the newly minted key in the space between them, held the twig-ridden dog against his nice suit jacket and let her decide.

Curiosity got the best of her.

She snatched the key and stomped up the steps.

Nathan stepped up on the porch and followed Monroe to the carved oak door. As she slid the key into the lock, his adrenaline exploded. Half of him feared what lay inside these doors. The other half had longed for this moment, though he'd been led to believe it could never happen.

The cowgirl turned and pointed to the pack of dogs, all following. "Stay out here. I'll be back."

Clinging to the curly black dog as if his sanity depended on it, Nathan followed Monroe through the door and into a spacious foyer leading into the great room. The musty scent of years rushed him. His footsteps, like echoes of the past, sounded loud in the abandoned house.

His heart rattled against his rib cage.

Directly in front of him, a curving staircase rose to the second floor. The staircase where he'd played with his toy trucks and peeked through the rails to the downstairs gatherings. And listen to his mother play piano.

He could almost hear the music and smell wood burning in the massive stone fireplace.

His gaze rushed from one spot to another. The enormous great room beyond the foyer. The study to the left beside the stairs.

Would Dad's paperwork still be there or had it been ransacked and taken as evidence by law enforcement?

To the right was the library with another fireplace, this one smaller but no less impressive. Dad had read to him in a big leather chair in front of that fire. Was that chair still there?

Emotion swelled inside him. Except for one, his memories were all good. Monroe, for all her cranky attitude, was right. What happened here was of human evil. This mansion held his happy childhood as well as the painful secrets he had yet to unravel.

"Are you just going to stand there and gawk?" Monroe's voice, surprisingly muted, jerked him out of his memories.

He nodded, hoping his expression didn't show the whirlwind spinning inside him. "I'm taking it all in. It's beautiful."

"Exquisite. I imagined it would look this way."

Again, her voice held the same awe he was feeling, though for different reasons. This house was not the bogeyman. For him, it was home.

He had to hold himself in check to keep from bounding up the staircase to his bedroom, the last place he'd seen his mother alive. She'd heard his prayers and tucked him in, smiling and tender as if nothing terrible would happen that night. He could almost feel her soft touch as she brushed back his hair and kissed his forehead.

The cowgirl pointed upward. "Cathedral ceilings and that chandelier. Wow. The people who built this had good taste as well as a lot of money."

Yes, they did. Which always brought him to the same question. Were finances the cause of his parents' deaths? Had they fought over money? Or had someone targeted the wealthy couple for robbery and made the break-in look like a murder-suicide?

Monroe's boots echoed on the dusty oak hardwood as she crossed into the great room and stood next to the fireplace. Dust motes danced in the sunrays beaming through the tall rows of windows on either side of her.

Nathan let her lead the way. He dawdled along, allowing the wispy snatches of memory to dance around the edges of his mind.

Mother had elaborately decorated that fireplace for every holiday. A spring wreath and religious symbols at Easter. Fall colors at Thanksgiving.

Flags in red, white and blue on July Fourth. At Christmas, Mother had gone overboard with lights, garland and stockings that bulged with mystery.

Someone had draped the furniture with plastic, but some items that he recalled were gone. He didn't know what had happened to them.

"Can't you imagine this fireplace all covered in garland and lit up at Christmas?" Monroe asked, as if reading his mind. "Maybe a nativity scene along the hearth. The tree must have gone right here beside it." She gestured up and down the tall row of windows. "A giant one, maybe a spruce, clear to the ceiling."

For once, the cowgirl sounded animated, interested, excited.

He knew then. Monroe Matheson of the bad attitude and massive chip on her shoulder might not like him, probably didn't like people in general, but she loved this house.

"Yes," he managed around a clogged throat.

Rake wiggled, wanting down. Realizing he must have been clinging too tightly, Nathan bent to release the pup.

"I wouldn't do that if I were you." Monroe scooped the dog up again. "He's not housebroken, and these floors are real hardwood. I'll put him out with the others."

"I'll explore." Without awaiting her response, Nathan followed the flowing floor plan into the long dining area where a chandelier dangled dusty and dull over a massive table. He'd rarely eaten there, so his memories of the space were vague.

Mother, Dad and he usually ate in the breakfast nook next to the bay window that looked out over Mother's butterfly gardens. She'd loved flowers and kept them all around the house, even in his bedroom.

He hurried through the butler's pantry, past the kitchen to the nook. Like everything else, the small round banquette table where he'd enjoyed breakfast for six years was covered in layers of dust. A simple blue vase, the flowers long ago disintegrated and turned to dust, sat in the middle.

Built-in seating, upholstered in sun-faded stripes, ran the length of the curving windows. Heedless of the dust and thick spider webs, Nathan lifted the top.

So much about the house, like that odd nagging in his gut, was vague, but he remembered this well. He'd called the bench his treasure chest. Inside, a jumble of toys looked as if a child had left them behind only yesterday.

"There you are."

At the voice, Nathan jumped.

Monroe chuckled. "Ghost stories getting to you?"

"I didn't hear you come in." He'd expected her

cowgirl boots to be noisy against the kitchen's stone flooring.

"You were deep in thought."

He could not deny it. "I can't help wondering about the people who lived here. Who were they beyond their names and the tragedy? What made them laugh or worry or feel sad? What were their hobbies, likes and dislikes? What was life like for them here in the house and on this guest ranch?"

Monroe was looking at him with that sideways stare of hers, hair covering one eye like an old-time movie star. "That's a lot of questions."

"Maybe, but aren't you curious, too?"

"I wouldn't be here if I wasn't."

Nathan allowed a smile to ease up through his emotional turbulence. He was beginning to understand some things about his cowgirl companion. Monroe couldn't give him an outright yes. She couldn't admit to caring. So she couched her words in attitude, even while admitting she wanted to know more about the house and the Vandivers.

"Since I plan to revive the guest ranch, I need to know everything I can. Marketing is essential to a business, and a tragic history draws tourists like ants to a picnic."

"You're going to focus on the murders?"

Inwardly, he winced every time *murder* was mentioned.

"No." Nathan shook his head. "I intend to bring

Persimmon Hill Guest Ranch back to what it once was, only better. I want guests to forget the bad and focus on all that's good and beautiful about this ranch."

He desired to revitalize Persimmon Hill Guest Ranch as he'd never desired anything since the day his parents disappeared from his life. Hereon lay peace, closure.

As if he'd said the words she'd needed to hear, Monroe spun toward him, expression full of pleasure, the first really open pleasure he'd seen in her. Her hair flew back from her face.

Monroe was, indeed, beautiful.

And from her hairline, across her left cheek and down her neck, one side of her face was badly scarred.

Chapter Three

Monroe realized her mistake when Nathan's silvery eyes registered shock.

She wanted to run and hide from this gorgeous man's appraisal. Someone with his good looks would find her monstrous, too terrible to behold.

But the Pandora's box had been opened, just as Nathan had opened the window seat. He'd seen the scars. About now, he'd be making up excuses to leave.

She'd almost liked this guy, if only because he cared about Persimmon Hill.

Jerking aside the long hair she used as a shield, Monroe defiantly displayed the full damage fire had done to her face and neck. She knew how the scars looked. Puckered. Lumpy. Discolored. No amount of plastic surgery could replace what was lost.

"Look your fill." She let the hostile tone tell him exactly how she felt about nosy, pitying strangers. "And then run like a scared rabbit away from the monster."

Nathan gazed at her for a long minute while she thought her heart would explode and she'd die of rage, humiliation and despair. If he said he was sorry or showed one smidgeon of pity, she'd do something terrible.

She braced for it, expecting the sympathetic platitudes and questions.

They didn't come.

The too-handsome man simply said, "No matter what I say at this point, it'll be the wrong thing. So let's go explore the rest of the house and property."

Monroe blinked enough times to blur her vision. She opened her mouth, shut it, opened it again. "Okay."

She added unpredictable to Nathan's list of characteristics. Not that she was keeping score or anything, but the man must be more than a pretty face. She was certainly more than her appearance. Had he realized this? That behind the damaged skin was a good brain and a once-nice person who tried to love Jesus, but found her faith floundering because she couldn't love herself anymore?

She didn't like giving the male species that much credit, nor did she like thinking she could be wrong, but Nathan seemed different.

His footfalls thudded above her on the stairs.

She glanced down the hallway leading in that direction. Nathan was running away, just as she'd expected.

Okay. Good. She could put him in her already stuffed box of worthless men who only cared about a woman's physical beauty.

Letting the anger take over, she stormed down the hall toward the staircase. She was going to see this house whether he liked looking at her or not.

"You coming?" he called over his shoulder, one hand on the oak-wood banister from halfway up the padded steps.

Some of her anger fizzled. He was waiting for her?

Confusing man.

Monroe broke into a quick step and caught up, mind jumbled, still off-balance from Nathan's reaction, but eager to explore this mansion that had held her imagination forever.

Nathan waited patiently on the landing atop the stairs, glad to leave the rest of the downstairs until later when he was alone. If he could ever bring himself to go inside that one particular room.

Monroe probably blamed his quick departure on her scars instead of the unexplored spaces he wasn't yet ready to see.

How had she been burned? When? Where?

She was clearly embarrassed by the change to

her appearance. He understood that, given the beauty of the other side. But she was still a very attractive woman.

Her attitude could use some work, but the scars did not change the appeal of her face and figure and quick mind.

"Wow, look at this space." She stopped at the top of the banister. "It's huge for an upstairs landing, isn't it? I wonder what they used it for."

He knew. Though the furniture had disappeared, the upper landing had been a rarely used seating area with colorful art, more of Mother's beloved plants, and a fancy mirror where she'd always stop for one last look before going out. The decorative mirror still hung on the far wall, casting a lonely reflection of the downstairs' vaulted ceiling.

From this point, the house divided into two wings. His parents had the left wing. His room and playroom had been on the right.

Not ready to enter his parents' rooms just yet, he turned right and began opening doors. Guest rooms, a game room, storage closets. So many rooms for such a small family. Had Mother and Dad planned for more? Did they expect to rent out the rooms as part of the guest ranch? Or was theirs simply the indulgence of the wealthy?

Reaching his bedroom, he pushed open the door and braced for another flood of nostalgia. It came in a rush.

His room was intact. The bedding was rumpled, just the way he'd left it, though clothing spilled from the drawers and closet as if someone had hastily packed a few things and rushed away. Which was exactly what had happened.

He'd felt safe and secure in this room. Had he been? Why Mother and Dad and not him?

The question haunted Nathan, driving him to find the answer.

Monroe came up beside him. "I'd almost forgotten they had a child."

"A boy," he murmured, catching himself before he revealed the rest. That he was that boy.

"My nephew would love that race car bed." Monroe pointed to the car-shaped bed where he'd imagined himself to be a world champion racer. "I'll have to tell Harlow about it."

Brain muddled, stomach swirling and heart racing like the toy cars he'd driven all over this colorful play rug, Nathan turned slightly to look at her. "Who's Harlow? Your family?"

She huffed and rolled her eyes. "What? You thought someone like me would be a recluse living in a cave?"

He'd stepped on her inner wounds again and activated the sarcasm. This time he didn't hold it against her. "How old is your nephew?"

Her ruffled feathers settled. She loosened her defensive stance. "Davis is five. The best little kid in the world, though I only see him half of

the year now that his mom and dad have a second home in Florida."

Five. Her nephew was so very close to the age
when Nathan's whole life had exploded. Nathan
hoped, no, he prayed, that nothing like that ever
happened to another child.

"Sweet age," he muttered. "Innocent."

"You have kids?"

She still tilted her head away from him when
she spoke as if he didn't know about the scars she
tried so desperately to hide. He wanted to tell her
that hiding wasn't necessary, at least with him,
but figured any mention of the scars could send
her into another tizzy.

So far, she was his best connection to the past,
through her parents. She was also a local and,
therefore, a source of information about the area.
Nathan didn't want to sever the tenuous connection.

"No kids." He took a toy from the row of
shelves along one wall. From long-ago muscle
memory, he transformed the bright red robot into
a fire truck. "I'd hoped to have one or two by now,
but it didn't happen."

"Your wife doesn't want children?"

Was this a subtle way of asking if he was married? Or the natural ebb and flow of conversation?

He replaced the truck on the shelf next to Mr.
Potato Head. His broken marriage still pained

and shamed him. He felt as if he'd let God down, though Clare had done the leaving.

"Divorced. You?"

"Never married." By the way her voice turned icy again, he figured there was more to the story than she was telling.

He was smart enough not to ask.

While he dawdled in the bedroom with memories of bedtime prayers and race track cars and hours of happily entertaining himself, Monroe peeked in the adjacent bathroom and walk-in closet.

"Fortunate kid to have his own suite."

"That boy would trade everything he had then and now to see his parents alive." He caught the somber tone and added, "Anyway, that's what I think."

"Me, too. It's terribly sad. I wonder what happened to him. Who raised him? If he had a good life after losing his parents in such a horrible way?"

"You're as curious as I am." He managed a smile when he said it.

She sniffed. "Never denied it."

His smile widened. Pushing the right buttons on Monroe's attitude could be almost entertaining.

Knowing he'd return to this room again later, maybe even sleep here, he walked out into the wide hallway where the long patterned runner had faded to obscure blues and browns.

They peeked inside another room or two before Monroe said, "I should check on the dogs. They get nervous if I leave them for too long."

"What's the story with all the dogs?" Ready to leave anyway before she mentioned the additional downstairs spaces, Nathan turned toward the staircase. Those were private places, for his eyes only.

"Strays."

Her reply surprised him. "All of them? How did that happen?"

"About a year ago, someone dumped a mama dog with three pups near our house. I found homes for them. After that, dogs seemed to appear with regularity. People must think I'm a sap."

She was. At least with animals. He wouldn't tell her that. Though her bark was clearly worse than her bite, Monroe was testy.

"And you take them all in? Why not the animal shelter?"

"Town shelters don't take rural animals. We're on our own. But it's okay. I can find homes for most of them through social media."

Tough cowgirl wasn't as tough as she let on.

"And the ones you don't find homes for?"

"Are outside wondering where I am."

She'd just told him so much about herself. Underneath the hard tortoise shell, Monroe Matheson was a woman who cared.

He motioned for her to lead the way down the stairs. "I think we've seen the bulk. The rest can wait." Some places were too private to enter with a new acquaintance. "I'll follow you out."

She shrugged as if she didn't care one way or the other. "Fine."

Holding to the golden-oak banister, Monroe trotted down. Nathan followed, eyes on the woman's back and narrow waist. The turquoise blouse, loosely tucked in above a leather belt with her name across on the back, fluttered with her movements.

The stir of attraction bumped against him again.

They reached the bottom floor and moved toward the front entry, both of them quiet as if contemplating what they'd seen and the people who'd lived and died here. He certainly was.

As they stepped outside into the sunshine once more, every single dog stopped exploring and perked its ears before bolting toward Monroe.

She went to a crouch, ruffling ears and saying, "Miss me?"

The big pit-looking monstrosity barreled against her and snuggled in, whining like a baby, his entire body wagging from side to side. Monroe tumbled backward onto the overgrown grass and laughed.

Nathan paused to watch and listen to the joy rolling from the cowgirl. Until now, she hadn't laughed. He had the random thought that a man could listen to that sound forever.

Perching on the edge of the porch, he enjoyed the scene as Monroe wrestled and played with the pack. Finally, Rake, the tangled mass of leaves and fur, decided he was outnumbered by the big kids and trotted over to Nathan, red tongue pulsing.

"Hello again, little one." He scooped the dog up in one hand and set the grassy mess of canine on his lap. Rake gazed up at him, black eyes shining. Nathan was convinced the dog was smiling.

Monroe untangled herself and joined them on the porch. The other dogs huddled around, vying for attention.

"I still haven't seen your horse." He picked a few leaves from Rake's fur.

"Buzz does his own thing, but he's around."

"Want to explore the outbuildings with me?"

The yellow retriever mix settled on Monroe's boot toe. The one-eyed dog seemed to consider human feet as her chair. Monroe rested a hand on the wavy ears. "I really should go home."

"Why?"

"Because I'm trespassing on some rhinestone cowboy's property. He might not like it."

"What if he promises not to press charges?"

"In exchange for my scintillating company?" She tossed her head and snorted. "If he's that desperate, I could be convinced."

He wasn't desperate, but she interested him, and her knowledge of his ranch and the adjacent town and its people could prove valuable. Having companionship on this journey, even that of a stranger with a bad attitude, made the explorations easier.

Six months kept hammering at the back of his brain.

He was good at his job, but was he that good?

"Come on," he coaxed, eager to get on with it. "You're curious about the rest of the property. Admit it."

"I'm avoiding jail time." She got up and dusted her hands down her jean-clad thighs. "If you're waiting on me, you're backing up."

On long, admirable legs, she and her pack started off without him.

Chuckling at her sarcastic wit and feeling as if he'd won a victory, Nathan, with Rake in hand, hurried to catch up.

"That long silver building is one of the main horse barns." Monroe pointed. "I've been in there. Also those two barns next to it."

Nathan gave her a mild look, resisting a smile. "Trespasser."

She made a face. "You wouldn't complain if you knew I nailed the sheet iron back on the roof after a storm came through."

He could see her doing that. "I stand corrected. Thank you."

"I didn't do it for you."

He laughed. What an entertaining woman. "You didn't even know me."

"I still don't."

With every snarky comment, Nathan's original somber mood lightened. Having Monroe Matheson around challenged and amused him in ways he hadn't expected and distracted him just enough to keep him from brooding about his past.

He'd been anxious about going inside the mansion alone. Her company had made it easier.

Five minutes inside and all his dread had evaporated. He belonged here. This was his dream now.

Together they explored the tack room, the feed room, two of the hay barns before heading to the aforementioned horse barn. Except for a few random tools, some dried-out tack and saddles, buckets and miscellaneous junk, the buildings were empty, though the smell of their original contents remained. Horses, feed, leather, hay. A mix and mingle of odors that declared this place a ranch.

In the horse barn breezeway, shot with sunlight from the end door and rows of high windows, Monroe upended a dirty white feed bucket and sat down. Stalls lined each side. He could envision equine heads peering with curiosity over the half-doors.

Except for Rake, who seemed enamored of Nathan, the pack of dogs explored every open stall, noses to the ground. The terrier bolted after something, likely a mouse.

"Are you serious about the dude ranch thing?" Monroe asked from her cowgirl's throne.

He was very serious. His entire future rested on the next six months.

Nathan leaned an elbow on the top of a stall door. The structures remained sturdy and well built, which meant less repair for him to worry about. The faster he could get the place up and running, the better.

"Guest ranch. *Dude* sounds derogatory."

"Oh, puhlease. In whose estimation?" Out of what Nathan realized was constant habit, she pulled at the side of her hair and covered her face. "If you're serious, you'll need to spend a lot of money."

She was correct. Money was at issue. Lots of it. If he failed to meet the deadline, he'd have to sell Persimmon Hill to repay the loan, and he might even lose his job.

He did not, of course, share any of those troubled thoughts with this interesting stranger.

"Investors know they have to spend money."

He wished she'd stop hiding the scars. They had jarred him at first, but not now. Nothing could detract from those stunning green eyes.

"So that's what this is all about? Investment property? You'll set up the guest ranch and leave others to run it?"

"For now, let's say I'm a hands-on kind of businessman." With this property, he was. He had no
choice. This was his baby, his past, his future. If
he could keep it.

He'd been happy on this ranch. He wanted that
back as much as he wanted to somehow discover
that his father had not murdered his mother.

Taking an even dirtier bucket from one of the
stalls, Nathan dusted the top and upended it on
the ground facing Monroe.

"Careful, cowboy," she said. "You'll mess up
your fancy suit pants."

He sat down anyway. "Here's what I envision.
Any and all advice from a *real* rancher—" he
paused to shoot her a grin "—is welcome."

"You want *my* advice?"

"You're a real cowgirl, aren't you?" He grinned
again, hoping to coax an answering grin. "Or did
you just find those boots?"

She sniffed at him, but he was pretty sure he
detected a twinkle in her eye. "I know my way
around a small spread like my family's couple of
hundred acres, but a ranch like this requires a lot
more than my small-time knowledge."

"Don't sell yourself short." He thought she
probably did that a lot because of the scars.

"What exactly do you want to do here?"

*Get to know my parents. Restore their dream
ranch along with their reputations. Prove to my*

grandparents that Persimmon Hill is not the evil place they believe.

Find closure.

But he only said, "Open up for guests the way it was once, except updated and better. Southeastern Oklahoma is a tourist destination, and tourists need a place to stay."

"That's true. The Kiamichi wilderness backs up to this property. Did you know that? All those forests, hills and lakes are a treasure trove of outdoor activities."

"Exactly. And why not give them something extra? Horseback riding, of course, but maybe ATVs to explore the wilderness. Hot tubs. Paddleboats for one of the bigger ponds. They can fish, hike the woods and creeks, maybe experience the day-to-day ranching operation."

"You'll need real ranch hands for that part."

"Once I get a construction crew in to repair and remodel everything, I'll put out a call for experienced cowboys." He tilted his head. "And cowgirls."

"You are *not* changing the house into some tacky tourist destination where people rummage through the mansion and mess things up."

She said it as if he had no choice.

"We'll see."

She stewed on that a little, digging her boot toe into the dirt floor.

Nathan relented. "I'm getting ahead of myself,

though. First, the inspector and general contractor. Then, I'll figure out what to do about the rest. What do you think?"

"It's a nice dream, Nathan."

His next idea was a long shot but he tossed it out there anyway. "Want to help me make it come true?"

One of the dogs—the squatty one with the bad sinuses—wandered out of a stall. Monroe wiggled her fingers toward it. "Come here, Gramps."

"Gramps?"

"He's old. Rejected, probably because of his age and constant snoring and allergies." To the dog, she said, "Getting tired, pal?"

Gramps plopped down beside her bucket with a congested sigh and a puff of dust.

The dog's appearance was so unfortunate, age was likely not the only factor that caused him to be rejected. Whatever his lineage, his wrinkled face was practically flat, his nose pushed up and in like a button too often pressed. Multicolored in browns and blacks with a skinny tail that didn't fit his squatty body, he looked like a stubby coffee table. It would take a special person to love Gramps.

Apparently, Monroe was that person.

Was she also the person he needed on this ranch? "So what do you say?"

"About what?"

"About coming to work for me."

"You don't know me. Why would you want me to?" The frown creased her entire face, puckering the forehead scars.

"I need someone who knows ranching, someone who can teach me what I need to know."

He didn't examine why he wanted it to be *this* cowgirl, but he did.

She made a disparaging noise. She was good at that. "You can't live long enough to learn everything you need to know about ranching."

"Maybe not, but I know business and construction. With a good teacher and experienced hands, I can learn enough about ranching to run a successful enterprise." Nathan jacked an eyebrow toward Monroe, goading her just a little. "Unless you're not really a cowgirl and can't handle the task."

She narrowed her eyes in warning. "Don't be snide."

He chuckled. "You won't have to teach me everything. I can ride a horse. I learned as a boy."

"Well, whoopee-do. Good for you. A regular Lone Ranger." She swirled a finger over her head like a lariat.

Lone Ranger. The moniker fit. He'd felt alone most of his life. His grandparents had hid so much from him that he was still sorting truth from avoidance and white lies.

"So what do you say? Help me get this place up and running. Maybe even stay on and be my front man—pardon me—front woman. Teach our guests the rudiments of riding and ranching? The work's hard but the boss is easy and the pay's excellent."

Monroe jerked to a stand, rattling the bucket in the process.

From the sudden, icy change in her demeanor, Nathan thought an arctic cold front had moved into the barn.

"Not interested." She snapped her fingers. "Dogs, come."

Before he could figure out what he'd said or done to spark such a reaction, Monroe walked out of the barn. The wheezing Gramps trotted along behind her. Rake looked from Nathan to his owner, bewildered.

"I'm confused, too, buddy," Nathan said.

From outside, he heard a shrill whistle, followed by the pounding hooves of a running horse. Her ride home, he assumed.

Raking more dirt and leaves into his fur, the straggly dog gave Nathan one last glance and raced after his owner, his short legs and missing paw a messy blur.

Nathan considered following, too, but decided against it.

Rising from his impromptu seat, he strode to the wide, open doorway.

Straight and tall in the saddle, Monroe, atop a

sleek chestnut horse, trotted away from Persimmon Hill. Her pack of dogs loped to keep up.

What had just happened?

And why did he care one way or the other if Monroe liked him or not? She was testy, difficult and downright rude.

With her attitude, she'd run off all his guests. He didn't need that.

Yet, Monroe Matheson intrigued him as no other woman had in a long time. And she was a connection, through her parents, to his past.

Somehow he'd offended her.

Pushing back his jacket, he perched a hand on each hip and watched until the blond head disappeared over a rise.

He'd messed up. He didn't know how, but he had.

His first good contact to his parents was gone.

Nathan breathed out a long, troubled sigh.

The mansion and his day planner awaited, along with dozens of tasks he needed to tackle, and tackle quickly.

He couldn't spend another minute wondering about Monroe Matheson.

Chapter Four

The five-mile ride back home gave Monroe time to process the strange encounter with Nathan Garrison.

Although she resented his intrusion on this nearly perfect June day, the man interested her. Part of her had always hoped someone would resurrect Persimmon Ranch. She certainly didn't have that kind of money. Apparently, Nathan did.

When he'd first asked her to work for him, she'd actually considered the offer. But only as a consultant while he got the ranch up and running. Certainly not as some object on display for his guests to see. Didn't the man have any sense at all? One look at her and guests would freak out and drive away.

Holding Buzz's reins loosely in one hand, she touched her cheek with the other. The destroyed skin reached from the hairline down her neck, shoulder and left arm. Clothing and hair could hide only so much.

A knot formed in her esophagus. She tried to swallow it but it stuck fast.

She'd never work in view of the public again.

Nathan Garrison would have to find someone else to be his "front" person. She couldn't be the front of anything.

Stopping near a pond to let the dogs catch up and grab a drink of water, Monroe dismounted and waited. Though she'd traveled a good two miles, she was still on Persimmon Hill land. With mountains framing the backdrop, puffy white clouds in the blue sky above and long patches of pasture broken by woods and ponds, the property was breathtaking.

She hoped Nathan didn't ruin the property by dividing it up. There weren't many acreages of this size left.

If she worked for him, she could lessen the chances by pointing out the value in keeping the full estate intact. Every single day.

Not happening. She didn't like him that much.

Except she kind of did. He hadn't bolted after seeing her face. One major point for the pretty boy.

The dogs, reenergized and shaking water from their fur, milled around her. Gramps, for all his snorting, refused to ride on horseback. The dog had his pride.

Fur tangled with twigs and leaves, little Rake was not as particular. Three short legs were fast but not as efficient as four long ones. He raised his front paws to Monroe's knees, black button eyes begging through a curtain of messy fur.

"All right, then. Up you go." With Rake in the crook of her elbow, she swung into the saddle and started home again.

When she rode into the barnyard of her family's small farm-ranch, Monroe experienced a thrill. A rental car was parked at the side of the house.

Her sister Harlow was home.

After quickly caring for the horse and leaving the dogs to their own devices, she hurried into the rambling old farmhouse she'd called home since she was ten years old.

A five-year-old slammed into her legs. "Auntie!"

Monroe squatted to face him. "Hey there, Davis, how's my favorite guy in the whole wide world?"

"Do you still gots dogs?"

"Tons of them." She gave his wiggling body a hug. "Out back."

"Yay!" The boy raced away. Monroe heard the back open and squeals of delight.

Smiling, she stood to hug her red-haired sister. Harlow, two years her senior, glowed.

"Wow, you look like a million dollars." Monroe held her big sister at arm's length. "Florida life agrees with you."

Since marrying her high-school crush and the father of Davis, a man who also happened to be a very successful professional athlete, happiness beamed from Harlow like a spotlight.

If she didn't love her sister so much, Monroe would have been jealous. But it wasn't Harlow's fault that Monroe would never have that kind of relationship.

"I wish the Florida sunshine would give me a tan, but..." Harlow shrugged and indicated one pale arm lightly dappled in freckles. "Not happening. You, on the other hand, should come home with me for a few weeks. A tan with your blond hair and green eyes would be beautiful. Lay on the beaches, swim, paddleboard, relax. You'll love it."

While in the navy Monroe had had her share of beaches, thank you. And looking beautiful was in her past. Harlow knew that but, bless her, she kept trying.

"Where's what's-his-name?" Monroe still pretended not to like Harlow's husband. He was male, which made him suspect.

Like Nathan Garrison. Too good-looking to trust. Except Nash Corbin seemed to be okay. He adored Harlow and Davis, which elevated him above swamp mud. Barely.

"Nash is up at the other place." Harlow jerked a

thumb toward the north and her husband's family ranch. She, Nash and Davis stayed there whenever they came home to Oklahoma. "Come in the kitchen. Poppy and I want to talk to you about something."

"That sounds ominous."

Harlow pumped her eyebrows. "I made strawberry shortcake."

"Ooh. Yes. Lead on."

Harlow went to the staircase and yelled, "Poppy, Monroe's home."

Knowing full well that Harlow had something on her mind besides dessert, Monroe, nonetheless, followed her into the eat-in kitchen.

Poppy, their eighty-something grandfather, dressed in blue jeans and long-sleeved snap-front shirt like the cowboy he'd always been, came into the room. Since finally agreeing to getting his knees replaced, he moved with less pain and no longer required a cane, but had slowed down considerably.

Even now, he insisted on wearing his heavy Western boots when athletic shoes would have been lighter and easier. With shock-white hair and a matching handlebar mustache, Gus Matheson was a throwback to the Old West. All he needed was a six-gun on his hip.

"Got something to tell you, Monroe." Holding to the armrests, he settled slowly on a chair. "Harlow, where's that folder?"

Monroe's curiosity rose. The last time someone had brought in a folder had been when Nash had paid off this ranch's double mortgage. As much as she didn't like men in general, she held a grudging respect for Nash Corbin. He took good care of Harlow and Davis. So far.

You never knew about men. They'd turn on you if something went wrong. Such as getting half your body burned off while fighting a fire that saved their sorry hide.

The anger started to simmer inside her again. Riding to Persimmon Hill always helped keep it at bay. One thought of her ex-fiancé, Tony Berg, and she was mad all over again.

Harlow, red hair pulled back in a long, sleek ponytail, opened a blue folder. "I'll get right to it. Poppy has decided to downsize the ranch, and I'm in agreement. He's selling most of the cattle and horses."

Shock reverberated down Monroe's spine. She couldn't have been more stunned if her sister had zapped her with a Taser.

"What? Why? This is our livelihood. We need cattle to make a living. You fought like a tiger to hold on to this ranch. What's wrong with you?"

"It's me, little sis." Poppy leaned both forearms on the table. "Except for a cow or two and a few horses for fun, I'm ready to sell out and retire. You girls don't need this place anymore."

"Yes, we do! I do."

He patted the top of her hand. "Now, don't get wire-twisted. This is your home and will be as long as you want it. But Harlow and Davis don't need it anymore. Taylor don't want it. She's still gallivanting all over kingdom come."

"Have you asked her?"

"Of course," Harlow put in. "I talked to her on the phone this morning. She was at a blue-grass festival somewhere in Kentucky." Harlow rolled her eyes. She remained frustrated by their younger sister's penchant for living footloose and fancy free. Taylor had barely arrived in time for Harlow's wedding before she'd left again. "She doesn't care what we do with the ranch."

"And I'm getting too far south of prime to wrangle cattle and farm equipment every day. Time to kick up my heels before I kick the bucket."

"I can take care of the cattle," Monroe insisted. "Go ahead and kick up your heels."

"No, ma'am. Time for you to get on with life."

"Poppy!"

"Now, hear me out." Between thumb and index finger, Poppy smoothed his mustache, a sign he was about to give a long speech. "Much as I appreciate your hard work and help on this ranch since you got home, I remember how much you loved your navy job. As I recall, you planned to continue firefighting right here in the Valley. But here you still are, hem-hawing around the mulberry bush and coddling an old man and his cows."

"You know I can't go back to firefighting. Not now."

"Why not?"

"You know why, Poppy!" Anxiety and dismay twisted in her gut like two strands of trouble. "I can't believe you'd do this to me."

Harlow grabbed her forearm, effectively shushing her as she spoke to their granddad. "Poppy, I want to talk to Monroe alone for a minute."

He nodded and Harlow tugged her to the back door and out into the cool, sunny afternoon.

Davis, romping with the dogs, waved from halfway to the barn. The two women waved back.

Harlow wasted no time getting to the point. Voice stern and stubborn, she said, "Monroe, calm down, stop thinking about yourself for a minute. That old man in there has given us his all since we were little kids. He's worked his tail off on this ranch to provide for us and never once complained. Now that we're all grown and perfectly capable of caring for ourselves, it's his turn to enjoy life the way he wants to."

Some of Monroe's steam cooled. She couldn't disagree.

Poppy had been the only family member to step up to parent three little girls when his only son and daughter-in-law died in a car accident. As far as she remembered, he'd never done anything just for himself. Everything had been for his three granddaughters.

"No one could have loved us better than Poppy," she conceded.

"That's right. And you know he's been seeing Ms. Bea down at the bakery. At their ages, no one but God knows how much longer they'll have. Poppy has earned a few years of enjoying himself with a lady friend without worrying about putting shoes on our feet or food on our table."

Again, she couldn't disagree.

"He needs me, Harlow."

"Of course he does. But he needs you to be okay without him, too."

Monroe sucked in a breath and turned to the side. "I can't think about losing him."

"Well, you'll have to at some point. We both will. But as he said, this home will always be yours as long as you want it. We aren't selling the property, just the livestock, which will give Poppy a nice income for the future. Please don't make him feel guilty about wanting to enjoy what life he has left."

Monroe sucked in a long, shaky breath and turned back to face her sister. "All right. I understand. Poppy deserves to do what he wants. He's earned that right over and over. I'm a grown woman. I'll figure out some way to make a living."

"There's money in the account for now and

you know Nash and I will help you until you find a job. That shouldn't be too hard to do in this economy."

Monroe stiffened. Like squatty old Gramps, she had her pride. "I will not take money from Nash Corbin."

Nor would she take a job in town where everyone could stare at her on a daily basis. And the fire department was out of the question. She didn't even want to fight fires anymore. She wanted... She didn't know what she wanted.

Harlow held up both hands. "Whatever. But right now, go back in there and tell Poppy you're happy for him. Can you at least do that?"

"Of course I can. I am!" She wanted Poppy to be happy. She hadn't realized he wasn't. But she wasn't happy for herself.

What in the world was she going to do now?

Nathan Garrison's offer slid through her thoughts. The way she saw it, she had two choices and one didn't count. Accept the drugstore cowboy's offer or apply to the local fire department, the way she'd once intended.

The thought of fighting fires terrified her now. She, the fearless one, was afraid of both the job and the stares.

Which left one choice. Work for the handsomest man she'd ever seen and be reminded every day of the contrast in their appearance.

Some choice.

* * *

This was where it had happened.

Nathan stood in the entry to the mansion's media room, blood rushing in his ears as he gathered the strength to step inside the last place his parents had been alive.

The dust-and-cobweb-laced room was in disarray as one would expect from a crime scene, but the worst had been cleaned away by someone.

"Thank you for that, Lord," he whispered, though cruel memories flashed like strobe lights through his brain.

The Lord had preserved Persimmon Hill and led him back here. Nathan was as sure of that leading as he was anything. But God never promised life would be easy. Being in this room certainly wasn't.

He sank into a chair away from the media couch where his parents liked to sit after he went to bed each night and watch a movie together.

The leather couch had to go. He couldn't look at it every day and not remember. In fact, he might do away with this room, remodel it completely into something else. Storage perhaps.

But that would come later, after he knew everything he could know about their deaths.

Had they been arguing that day? Had he felt any tension between them? Or noticed anything unusual?

Nathan dropped his head and squeezed his temples between his hands. He couldn't remember.

Rising, he crossed to the big-screen TV and pressed the eject button on the DVD player. After the usual whirr and pop, he removed the disc and read the label. They'd been watching one of Dad's action movies. Dad had loved the fast action, wild car chases and Western shootouts.

Nathan remembered that, though he didn't know why.

Other than flickering images and that one, last horrific sight in this room, his childhood recollections were mere feelings. Love. Security.

So why had Dad done what law enforcement claimed he'd done?

Stomach rolling until he thought he might be sick, Nathan quickly exited the room and locked the door behind him. He'd need more time and distance before he could go in again.

What good did looking do anyway? He wasn't a crime scene analyst and this crime scene happened too long ago to offer any clues to what occurred here. Any except the official ruling.

His cell phone jangled. Nathan fished the device from his pocket, glanced at the caller ID and felt his spirits lift.

"Carter, hello," he said into the receiver.

Carter Branch, his cousin and best friend, was the only person ever willing to discuss Nathan's past. At a year older, they were as close as the brother Nathan never had, and he trusted Carter with everything, even his dream of reopening Persimmon Hill.

"Did you make it safely to the ranch?"

"Spent last night here."

"How is it?"

"Not as bad as I expected, but restoration will take time and money. I'll have to move fast to make this happen by September."

"What will you do if you don't make the deadline?"

"The only thing I can do short of bankruptcy. Put Persimmon Hill up for sale and hope the property sells quickly so I can repay the loan and get back to a real-world job instead of a dream."

"Nothing wrong with having dreams, Nathan. I'm still shocked that the ranch was yours all this time and no one told you."

Even before the lawyer's startling call on his thirtieth birthday, he'd fantasized about coming home to Persimmon Hill again, about recreating the guest ranch his father had worked to establish. Carter knew that.

"You know how Granddad and Grandmother are. Silence is golden. If they didn't talk about it, maybe I'd forget about what happened." His breath huffed softly. "Like that was possible."

"They did the best they could. Remember, they lost a daughter in a horrible manner."

"I know. I know." He loved his grandparents. He just didn't understand them. "But they made me believe the ranch had been sold. I'll need a lot of help from God to forgive them for that."

"I don't understand their motives, either, Nathan, but they're good people. They must have thought Persimmon Hill was too traumatic to revive."

"They didn't want me here. That's for certain. Grandmother cried when I told her was coming here and Grandpa pleaded with me not to. The secrecy only made me more determined."

"Are you planning to dig into your parents' death records or focus on the restoration?"

"Both."

"Do you have time for that now? Shouldn't you wait until you know if the ranch can be revived in time?"

"That's exactly why I can't wait. If the ranch has to be sold, digging into their pasts will be even harder. The reasons for what happened that night have to be here, on the ranch, probably in this house."

He'd worried the idea in his head so much he got migraines. Someone somewhere knew a lot more than he did, and since the tragedy occurred at Persimmon Hill, it stood to reason that this is where he'd find answers.

"If I can get some time off, I'll drive down and help out. I can still swing a hammer like we did in college."

He and Carter had worked handyman and construction jobs to put themselves through college. They knew a thing or two about construction. It was crime investigation where both were clueless.

"I'd be glad for the help but mostly for the company."

"Lonely down there?"

Monroe Matheson flashed through his head. "Met an interesting woman yesterday."

"Oh, yeah?" Carter chuckled. "She must be pretty for you to mention her."

"She's beautiful, in a way, but man, does she have an attitude. She's a real-life cowgirl. I tried to hire her to teach me more about ranching, but she blew me off like so much dandruff."

Carter laughed out loud. "Nathan, my man, the last thing you need is a troublesome woman."

"Got that right. Been there and do not want to go back. I'm only interested in the cowgirl because she knows ranching."

"And she's pretty."

"Pretty interesting. She has a pack of dogs and every one of them is handicapped." It hit him then. They were all "damaged" in some way like she was. He did not tell that to his cousin. "Anyway, enough about Monroe."

"Oh, ho, so it's Monroe, is it? You already know the lady's name?"

"Leave it, Carter. I don't have the time or the heart to get involved with a woman."

"I hear that. The clock is already ticking."

His gut churned at the reminder. He needed an antacid bad.

"Defaulting on a loan would be a credit disaster I can't afford, but I stand to lose more than the money and Persimmon Hill."

"Your job." Carter knew the stipulations. Nathan had taken a leave of absence from his job as well as borrowed money against Persimmon Hill.

"I've spent years working my way up in the company. I have to get back there ASAP." More worry. He had to get back to his job. He had to complete the restoration. He needed to hire employees.

And he wanted to avoid hurting his grandparents any more than he already had.

The acid in his belly ate a little deeper.

"I sure wish I had the money to help you out."

"I know you do, buddy, and I'm grateful." Carter had a big heart and a small pocketbook. Generous to a fault, when he did have any money, Carter tended to give it away to someone in need. The man lived in a camper that he shared with a homeless person on a regular basis.

"When I get this ranch up and running, I'll have a place for you," Nathan said. "You can come up here, work with me, live on the property."

Carter's deep chuckle rumbled over the line. "Cuz, I don't know one end of a horse from another."

"I don't know much more than that. I'm trying to hire someone to run the ranching end while I handle the restoring and the business portion."

"Marketing and business you can do. I don't see you wrangling cattle."

"I'll learn. I always wanted to be a cowboy like my dad."

They talked a few more minutes. Carter listened as Nathan worried out loud and planned his day. Good man.

Nathan would be lost without God and Carter.

When the call ended, he made his way to the kitchen, where he'd stocked up on food and supplies yesterday afternoon following his interesting encounter with Monroe. Nathan drew a glass of water from the refrigerator spout and drank deeply. He'd had a time getting things back in working order, but the handyman in him wouldn't quit last night until he had.

He was thankful for the distraction of Carter's conversation, but his hands still trembled from looking inside the media room. They'd been shaking that final morning, too. In fact, his entire body had shaken for days afterward and he'd screamed with nightmares.

That he remembered well.

Thankfully, last night in one of the guest bedrooms had brought only sleep. Maybe his wasn't the most restful sleep but no nightmares had disturbed him. He had, however, tossed awhile, planning his next moves.

Before Carter's call, he'd already made phone calls this morning to an engineer, an inspector and a builder.

Surprisingly, two of the three had agreed to meet this week, a rare occurrence back in Houston, where permits and professionals took weeks to acquire. Once he had their input, he could move forward.

His stomach still churning, Nathan started up the stairs to rummage through his bags for antacids.

A dog barked.

Nathan paused, one hand on the banister, and turned toward the tall double entrance.

He didn't own a dog.

Before he could reach the peephole, the doorbell chimed.

Monroe Matheson stood on his porch. The pack of dogs circled her. The handsome chestnut horse, reins trailing, grazed on the too-tall grass.

Nathan's mood lifted. Decked out in a white hat, a gauzy blouse of Native American design, snug jeans and the same turquoise-and-brown boots, the intriguing cowgirl had come back.

Right now, he could use the company. Even if she carried a chip on her shoulder and had a sassy mouth.

He yanked the door open.

Before he could say a word, the cowgirl struck an insolent pose. "Wouldn't you know it? *Himself* is still here."

Comment dry as August in the desert, her pale green eyes, nonetheless, snapped with something he thought might be humor.

Nathan grinned. "You missed me."

"I loathe you. I like this house." Suddenly, she stopped her flow of sarcasm to frown at him. "You don't look so hot. You're white as a sheet. What's wrong?"

He tapped his belly. "Indigestion."

Her one visible eyebrow hiked. "Can't take your own cooking?"

"What cooking?"

She laughed. If he'd known poking fun at himself would bring that on, he'd have started earlier.

"Clearly, you need someone around who knows what they're doing."

"I do indeed. You volunteering? The job's still open."

"You said the work's hard and the pay's good. Let's talk about that."

He stepped to the side and motioned her through the double doors. A waft of sunshine and spice trailed the long-legged cowgirl into the foyer. Spice, not flowers. The fragrance suited her. She was definitely spicy.

"You uncovered the furniture." She slid a hand over the top of the long sofa.

He thought of a snappy reply about living with plastic furniture, but kept the thought to himself. She was the sassy one.

"Want some refreshment?"

"Sure. What do you have?"

"What do you want?"

"I want a lot of things, but right now, I'm feeling sorry for a greenhorn who's bought a ranch and doesn't know what to do with it. Call me a sap, but I'm compelled to help him. It's my Christian duty."

He latched on to that piece of commonality. "You're a Christian? Me, too. Maybe you can recommend a good Bible-believing church."

"I might. Depends on the pay around here." She smiled, an expression that tugged at the scar on the left corner of her mouth but still managed to add to her appeal. "About that refreshment. Got iced tea? It's hot out there."

"Tea bags."

As if she'd been in the house a hundred times instead of only once, she led the way to the kitchen. "Where?"

He opened the cabinet next to the sink and took down the new box. "I like it strong and sweet."

"Bless my soul. And here I pegged you for a sissy greenhorn."

"I'm full of surprises." He took the tea bags from her and put the water on to boil.

"Too bad. I hate surprises."

He grinned. Monroe Matheson amused and challenged him in ways he couldn't explain. One thing he knew, though, having her around took his mind off his troubles. A little. "What *do* you like, Monroe, besides sweet tea?"

"Dogs, horses, *privacy.*" Widening her eyes, she gazed around the room and up at the tall ceiling. "I like this house, but the cobwebs up there have to go. How did you stay here last night with all the spiders, dead bugs and mouse droppings?"

"Maybe I'm not such a sissy boy after all." He let that sink in.

One insolent shoulder twitched. "We'll see."

"Can you recommend a housecleaning service?"

"Oh, I'm full of recommendations. But let's talk duty and pay first, shall we?" With feminine grace that belied her tough-girl attitude, she slid onto one of the barstools.

Nathan pulled a stool around to face her. "Pay is commensurate with duties, which I outlined yesterday before you got mad about something and stormed off."

"I wasn't mad and I didn't storm. But I *was* a tad rude, and Poppy taught me better, especially if you're going to be my employer." She showed her teeth. "Be nice to the boss."

"Poppy?"

"My grandfather. He raised my sisters and me on his ranch."

"I was raised by my grandparents, too."

"Well, look at us. Two peas in a pod." She hopped off the stool to toss the tea bags into the pot of boiling water.

"What did I say yesterday that upset you so much?"

With her back turned, she rummaged in his cabinets until she found a pitcher and stuck it under the faucet. He'd already rewashed and rinsed all the dishes but didn't stop her. She seemed to need movement.

"I will not," she declared in a tone that left no question about her feelings, "be an object for people to stare at. I work in the background. Got it?"

So that was it. The scars. He noticed them, but she did such a good job of hiding the injury behind her hair that he quickly put it out of his thoughts. She, apparently, never forgot for a second.

"Understood. You set the terms."

"Where's the sugar?"

He got up from his barstool and got it for her.

"How did you get to be a successful businessman if you let employees call the shots?"

"I'm making an exception with you."

"Why?"

He wished he knew.

"Because I'm the boss, and I can." He grinned. She grinned back, apparently liking his sass as much as she liked her own. "We'll need horses. Good, broke horses that a kid can ride."

She nodded, brisk and businesslike. "I can gentle any that need work. Horses are my thing. Yates Trudeau is the best horse trainer in the county, but he only does ground work these days. I do it all."

He was hoping she'd say that. "I have my eye on a ranch sale next week."

"Good place to start. Ranch horses have been ridden almost daily and know their manners. I won't need to do much to tune them up for guests."

He knew that. He also knew a lot more than she gave him credit for about running a hospitality business. There was no need, however, for her to know his time crunch.

"About the pay." He named a sum that raised her eyebrows.

"Consider me on the clock," she said. "Grab a pen and paper. We'll make lists and get this rodeo started."

He was hoping she'd say that.

Chapter Five

"It's amazing what money can do."

Monroe paused in leading a blaze-faced gelding toward the tack room to admire the progress buzzing around Persimmon Hill like a swarm of honeybees.

Nathan Garrison could make things happen fast. Every day when she arrived, something new and different was happening on the guest ranch. He seemed in a hurry, as if he was on a fast-track mission to get things done before the world ended.

Being a businessman, he was probably thinking that time was money and the sooner Persimmon Hill Guest Ranch was up and running, the quicker he'd get a return on investment.

The man was definitely dumping a chunk of change into this place. He must be even wealthier than his expensive boots and hat said he was.

If she wasn't so paranoid about encountering

strangers, she'd have been excited about the progress. Nathan certainly was, as was her family when they'd learned about her new job as head wrangler and assistant to the big boss.

This morning, workmen crawled all over the buildings at Persimmon Hill. Large equipment Monroe couldn't even name broke the country quiet, moving lumber, bringing in concrete and gravel, smoothing dirt. One excavated the old swimming pool. Another dug trenches to install cables to all the cabins. Two huge tractors mowed the acres surrounding the house and other buildings. A baler rumbled along behind and spit out giant rolls of hay.

The place was a noisy hive of activity.

Monroe was happy to stay aloof with the horses and watch it happen. Nathan, on the other hand, was everywhere. Friendly as one of her dogs, he'd quickly become a popular figure with the workmen. Sometimes he jumped right in to help.

Imagine. Pretty boy getting his hands dirty, swinging a hammer or on the end of a shovel. He didn't seem in the least fazed by sweat and dirt and spider webs.

Had she misjudged him? Maybe. Not that her opinion mattered.

The golden boy with plenty of money, a charming personality and a perfect life was nothing to her but a good paycheck.

He'd be a dandy guest ranch host when the

time came. People would come here just to be around him. Especially the ladies.

And her dogs. Little Rake trailed him like a bloodhound. Often, she'd look up from working with the new horses to see the messy mutt tucked beneath one of Nathan's arms, rescued from being crushed by heavy machinery or falling sheet metal.

In a matter of days, the mansion got a fresh coat of paint in a soft yellow with white trim. The shutters were flung wide, and the windows and interior cleaned to a sparkle. The cabins and outbuildings were in various stages of repair and remodel.

Amazing, she thought. "Absolutely amazing. All because of money and a can-do will."

Sweaty and hot, Monroe patted the new horse and returned him to a stall. With practiced ease, she untacked and turned him out before heading toward the house to cool off with a tall glass of God's good water, as Poppy would say.

Funny, she thought. Now, that Persimmon Hill was coming back to life and she was busy earning a living again, she wasn't quite as angry at God as she had been. She had a ways to go and her face would never win another beauty contest, but being on the outs with the Creator of the universe was clearly a problem. Poppy claimed Jesus's strong arms would be open when she was ready.

She believed that. She just wasn't ready. Going to church was one thing, but living a Christian life quite another. She'd learned that from Poppy, too, as well as from hard experience. Some people who claimed to be Christians didn't bear any Christ-like fruit, another of Poppy's sayings.

The wolf pack, as she termed the five stray canines, emerged from various places around the horse barn and raced to catch up with her. Dust swirled around them like a cloud.

She paused long enough to ruffle ears and pat heads before continuing on.

As she entered the back door, Monroe breathed in the scent of painted walls, though the interior paint crew had moved out three days ago. Fresh color revitalized the old mansion, giving back some of its former glory. Clearing away the spider webs helped, too.

They still had a long way to go before the ranch was ready for guests, but Nathan's living quarters were mostly livable.

Tapping across the terra-cotta tile to the kitchen, Monroe felt grateful that Nathan allowed her to come and go anywhere on the ranch. At least for now, while work was in progress. She didn't know why he trusted her, and the notion made her uncomfortable at times.

Monroe was determined to be worthy of that trust.

She had quickly discovered that the man with

movie-star looks knew a substantial amount about construction and running a guest ranch. He had trades and professionals lined up like dominoes so not a moment was wasted.

He was a good boss. As cautious as she was about getting involved with people, especially male people, she sort of liked the guy. As a boss. Maybe as a neighbor.

Dealing with the sudden jolts of attraction was a problem, but she stomped them out with a well-placed bit of sarcasm and a hearty reminder of the danger of falling in love.

"Hey." A voice intruded her thoughts.

Monroe hunched her shoulders and pulled her hair across her cheek before turning around. Workmen frequently appeared out of seemingly nowhere so she was always on guard. "Oh, it's only you."

Nathan's charming smile flashed. He patted his left chest. "Your joy in seeing me each day fills my soul with delight."

She rolled her eyes. "I live to serve."

Uncomfortably aware of his good looks and of the fact that she was sweating worse than a glass of iced tea at a Fourth of July picnic, Monroe opened the oversize refrigerator and took out a bottle of water.

"Here you go." She offered it to him. "I'm buying."

"So generous. Thanks. Just what I came in here to get."

She reached back inside for another and thought about standing in the cool air for an hour or two. The cold dried the sweat on her face and distracted her thoughts of Nathan. A little. Nothing could make her forget how handsome he was and how awful she looked.

Uncapping the bottle, Monroe took a long swig, still basking in the refrigerated air. When she finally closed the door and turned around, Nathan was gone.

Well. That was rude.

Or was it?

She touched her cheek. Did she look especially scary today? Probably smelled like a horse, too. Had she turned his stomach so he couldn't even enjoy a drink of water?

Readjusting her hair again to cover as much as possible, she leaned against the granite countertop and pressed the cold, damp bottle against her forehead.

She'd been in a positive mood while exercising the horses.

So much for that.

Her cell phone chirped. Fishing it from her back jeans pocket, she read the text. Her heart squeezed. The positive mood was back.

What a kind thing for him to do.

Unused to favors, she nonetheless had to acknowledge when she received one. Or at least, she thought it was a favor.

Threading her way over polished hardwood and classy new area rugs, she poked her head into each first-floor room. All except the one he kept locked.

Where had he gone?

Office, probably.

Nathan spent as many hours in that cushy office as he did outside with her and the workers. He spent so much time on his cell phone, the device should be surgically attached to his head. Most of the time the video chat wouldn't work out here in the country, which frustrated him, but at least he had basic phone service.

He'd need a dependable landline at some point.

Monroe rapped a knuckle on the closed door.

"Yes?"

She pushed it open and stepped inside. "It's me. Thank you."

"For what?" He rolled his chair backward from the glass-covered executive desk. An opened folder and newspapers were scattered across the surface.

She held up her phone. "Harlow texted me. You bought Poppy's livestock."

She'd mentioned they were downsizing their family ranch when she'd agreed to work for him.

He shrugged as if it didn't matter. It did. "A

ranch needs cattle and horses. Yours were for sale."

Poppy's, not hers, were for sale, but she didn't correct him. He knew the ranch wasn't technically hers. "Livestock can be bought anywhere."

"You said the animals were healthy, the horses dead broke."

"And you took my word for it." A little quiver of *something* ran through her. She didn't like it one bit. Nor did she appreciate that tingly, itchy feeling that started up in her chest again.

He was her boss. She was a hired hand. No tingles allowed.

"That's why I hired you," he said. "You're a straight shooter who knows horses and cattle and this area of Oklahoma. I know business and construction. We're a team."

A team. And he'd called her a straight shooter. She was, but that he recognized her propensity for direct honesty ruffled her cynic's feathers. No guy was this nice.

The man was messing with her equilibrium. To get things back on track, she searched for something snarky to say.

"Well, big shot, you overpaid." Probably out of pity, which erased the tingles faster than they'd arrived. "You should have checked the market first."

"I did," he said mildly, his golden head tilted slightly to one side as he studied her. "Factoring in hauling expenses, vet checks and other expenses, I'd say I made a good deal. Your grandfather agreed to move the animals and help you keep an eye on them until a foreman is hired. They're already vet approved, most of the cows due to deliver calves this fall. That's two for the price of one. A win in my book."

He might be a greenhorn but he was nobody's fool.

"Still. Okay. Well." She shifted, uncomfortable, before choking out the words. "I appreciate the gesture. For Poppy's sake."

One less thing for Poppy to deal with as he pared down to the number of animals he wanted to keep.

"Business is business. He's happy. I'm happy."

But she could tell by his expression that he was pleased with himself and with her reaction.

Keeping her family's livestock, especially the three aging horses, from the sale barn and unknown destinations meant a lot to her. She was a softy about her animals.

Having endured all the gushy she could handle for one day, Monroe started to leave when something caught her eye. An old black-and-white newspaper photo of the Persimmon Hill mansion. "What's this?"

Moving closer to the desk, she saw the caption. She also saw Nathan's face. His expression had gone from pleased to intense. And more than a little closed off.

"Research on the property," he said.

"Right. You want to use the murders as promo."

"I don't." His tone was terse, harsh.

Monroe held up one hand. "Don't bite my head off. It was your idea."

"Didn't mean to snap." He took a breath and leaned back in the leather chair, one hand resting on the photo. "I intend to use the *history* of the guest ranch, not the tragedy. From reading the old guest book I found in the library, I learned that quite a few well-known people stayed here. Politicians. Celebrities seeking solitude. They even filmed part of a Western movie on the property. Did you know that?"

She didn't. She'd barely been old enough to be alive back then. "Really? That's interesting."

As much as she preferred to keep a cynic's distance, everything about Persimmon Hill and the man who owned it intrigued her.

Step carefully, cowgirl, or you'll step in something you'll regret.

"The few newspaper articles from that time only cover the deaths." Leaning forward again, his shoulders tense, he wore an expression she couldn't quite define. "That's wrong. People, even dead people, deserve better than that. They were certainly more than that one final tragedy."

As he spoke, his handsome face grew more intense and troubled as if he had a personal stake in changing public perception. In a way, she supposed, he did, since he intended the ranch to be an income-producing enterprise.

Still, Monroe couldn't help wondering what went on behind those silvery eyes. Being financially invested in the guest ranch comeback was one thing, but Nathan really threw himself into a project.

"Maybe instead of reading lurid news accounts that upset you, you should talk to people who actually knew the Vandivers."

He slid the article into the folder and closed it. "I intend to once I discover who they are. Would your parents be willing to meet with me?"

"My parents? Nathan, I told you my granddad raised me and my sisters. My parents died in a car accident when I was ten." Losing them was a pain that lingered in her heart and always would. Poppy had literally been God-sent to raise her and her sisters, but the ache for Mom and Dad never went away.

Nathan's shoulders slumped. Ruffling the top of his hair in aggravation, he blew out a sigh. "Somehow I let that slip past me."

His letdown was so obvious, she felt sorry for him and couldn't keep from saying, "I'll ask around about the Vandivers' other friends and find out who's still in the area that might talk to you. My grandpa wasn't close to them and may not know much, but I'll ask him."

"You'd do that? It would mean a great deal to me, Monroe. I'm serious. A very great deal."

One hip lower than the other, Monroe intentionally rolled her eyes. This conversation was getting way too touchy-feely. "Don't slobber. I'd do the same for anyone."

Her snarky comment was apparently just what Nathan needed. He smiled.

And, of all things, *she* felt better.

Two mornings later, Nathan spread his notes, a stack of prospective employee applications, and the plans for remodeling the lodge on the small table inside the sunroom. He added a yellow notepad with notes he'd made about people who might have known his parents. Some of the construction workers, he'd learned, enjoyed talking. The older ones were particularly informative, though much of what he'd heard about the previous owners of Persimmon Hill was purely gossip.

Through the sparkling-clean windows, his mother's gardens, long dead like her, spread before him and to his left toward the breakfast nook, overgrown and ugly. He wouldn't have the funds for a gardener, but Mother's gardens were something he wanted to do himself anyway, a tribute to the gentle woman he remembered.

Time was a factor. Always, always a factor, pressing at him like a weight that got him up at dawn and kept him awake long into the night.

Planting flowers took time he didn't have. The gardens could wait.

Did Monroe know anything about flowers?

Hands in his pants pockets as he gazed across the land of his birth, he pondered the prickly cowgirl. In the short time they'd worked together, he'd come to respect her. Beneath that tough facade was a quick mind and a hard worker with good ideas and a kinder heart than she wanted anyone to know.

He liked her. She tolerated him.

From here, he spotted Goldie, the one-eyed retriever mix romping with the sissy pit bull. Peabody, she called the battered pit, which made Nathan smile. A dignified name for a very undignified dog.

The presence of the pack could mean only one thing.

Nathan glanced at his watch. Monroe was on time. As always.

A carafe of coffee and two cups awaited his assistant's arrival. Although he'd never actually give her the title, Monroe had proved invaluable, as well as entertaining. She kept him on his toes.

"What good is a sunroom without plants?" Her voice turned him toward the entry.

Mouth curving at Monroe's abrupt way of saying good morning, he waved her inside. "Definitely. I was just thinking along those lines."

"Great minds, and all that nonsense." She tossed a hand as if shooing a fly.

In her usual Western boots, a pair of worn, boot-cut jeans with rips in the knees, a V-neck pullover printed with colorful Native feathers and, surprisingly, a Bible verse, Monroe was ready to work.

She wasn't lazy. In fact, she was a take-the-world-by-the-horns-and-get-things-done kind of person.

He was the same.

If he told her that, she'd repeat the "peas in a pod" comment with her usual sarcasm.

Some days he thought she liked him, at least a little. Most days he remained off-balance. Not that he let on. From living with his grandparents, he'd learned to go with the flow and take anything life gave him.

Except when it came to Persimmon Hill and his parents. He would not accept the general consensus until he knew for certain what had occurred that fateful night.

"There's a plant nursery on the south side of town," Monroe was saying. "You can buy or order anything you want there."

"Let's go there this afternoon." He didn't know why he'd said that. He didn't have time for this yet. Landscaping could wait.

Monroe shook her head. "You go. I have work to do."

So did he. Tons of it. Yet, resurrecting Mother's gardens pressed at him today for some reason.

He'd already seen the way Monroe budgeted the tack orders for the stable and chose quality at the best price. He could use that no-nonsense approach to purchases, especially when it came to Mother's gardens. He might let sentiment override his better judgment.

Was she reluctant to go with him because of the scars? Or because of him? At varying times, she seemed prickly about both.

Must be him. Surely, she ventured out into public on a regular basis.

"We'll see." He motioned toward the coffee carafe. "Grab a cup and let's talk."

She filled the mug, laced it with cream and settled in across from him as she did each morning. Another thing he'd learned about Monroe. She was a great listener.

Like his mother.

The thought came from out of nowhere.

"What's on the agenda?" she asked.

He reeled off a list of work that would happen today. "I'm keeping my eye on that plumber."

"I noticed the shoddy workmanship in a couple of places. Fire him. There are other good plumbers in the area."

"He has a wife and four kids."

"Then, he should work harder to keep this job. I guarantee no one else is paying him as well."

"I'll have a talk with him today."

Second chances. He believed in them. God had given him more than one in his life, and wasn't he currently searching for a second chance for his parents?

"Softie." Monroe spoke without her usual cynicism.

She was a softie, too, in some ways. Getting through that hard shell of hers required nothing more than a stray dog or an old horse.

With people, however, the guard wall was a regular fortress.

They went over the other details of the day. Nathan felt a certain satisfaction in discussing the work with Monroe. She loved the ranch and whenever she'd let it show, she was excited about the rapid progress. So was he.

So far, he was on schedule. A project this vast demanded it.

"What's the yellow pad for?" She tapped a fingernail on it.

"People list." He flipped to the previous sheet. "The construction foreman, Gene, lived in Sundown Valley back in the day. He didn't run in the same social circle with the Vandivers, but he recalled a couple of people who did."

"Are they still around?"

"He says they are." Nathan perused the list. Two names were a start. "Wayne Klondike and Rebecca Sandberg. Do you know them?"

"We're acquainted. Or used to be before I went into the Navy. This is a small town. Everyone knows everyone, at least by name."

It was the first he'd heard of her military service. Was that how she'd been burned?

He knew better than to ask. If she wanted him to know, Monroe would tell him. If she didn't, she'd cut him off at the knees and walk out.

He couldn't let that happen. He needed her.

"Do you know where these people live?"

"Vaguely, but Ms. Bea at the Bea Sweet Bakery knows everyone in the county. She'll have addresses. She may even be friends with them."

His mouth quirked. "Everyone in the county?"

"Clearly, you have not met the amazing Ms. Bea. Nor her talented pastry chef, Sage Trudeau. People come from miles to buy sweet rolls or specialty breads at the Bea Sweet." She aimed a pointer finger at him. "And don't go falling in love with Sage. She's easily the most beautiful woman you'll ever see, but one of the Trudeau boys snatched her up a while back."

Monroe averted her face as if the mention of a beautiful woman reminded her of the scars.

Sage Trudeau might be beautiful, but he was looking at a woman who intrigued him for more reasons than her beauty.

Tamp it down, buddy. You have a goal and a purpose at Persimmon Hill that does not include romance.

"Does the bakery serve food?" he asked.

"Light fare, why?"

"Great. It's a date, then. We'll grab lunch, sample all the sweet rolls we can eat and have a chat with Ms. Bea. Then, you can show me where the plant nursery is."

With the construction manager on-site today, he could afford a few hours.

Monroe's expression shuttered. She looked down at her coffee mug. Nathan felt her tension all the way across the table.

"I told you already, Nathan. I have too much work to do."

"But I'm your boss and I decide what work needs to be done and what can wait."

Monroe said nothing but the daggers hitting him between the eyes said plenty.

He tried again.

"People in this town don't know me, Monroe. You're my intro. I need you with me."

"No can do. Sorry." She started to rise. "You go on your little excursion alone. Horses don't train themselves."

Nathan knew what she was doing. Running away from the fear of stares, of pity. He'd seen her duck inside a barn or hurry away when workers came near. The times she had to speak to one of them, she'd turn sideways and gaze toward the distance.

He caught her wrist. Slender, but strong, like her.

"Monroe," he said softly. "Don't run away from me. Please."

She stared down at his fingers wrapped around her wrist but didn't pull away. "You can't possibly understand."

"Maybe more than you realize."

She snorted. "Spare me the poor-little-rich-boy scenario and go look in the mirror."

Rich? He wasn't. This entire project would be easier if he'd inherited money along with the property. He hadn't. Any funds his father had left him had long since been used to pay taxes and insurance. "People can carry scars on the inside, too."

Her body, leaning toward the door a moment ago, relaxed.

Though she was no longer trying to leave, Nathan was reluctant to release his hold. Touching Monroe's smooth, soft skin sent warmth curling through him.

For several years, since his divorce, he'd sleepwalked through the occasional date, feeling nothing. Suddenly, a sassy, hard-edged cowgirl with a chip on her shoulder stirred his interest.

Not a good plan at the moment for many reasons.

He let go of her arm, curling his fingers into his palm.

"Better scars on the inside than on the outside

for the whole world to stare at." But her words were soft, tempering the usual scorn.

"Really? And you know this with certainty?"

"I'm not going with you out into public, Nathan. I know we both lost our parents as kids. We have that in common and, yes, it still hurts. But obviously, you've done all right in life."

"For me, it was more than losing my parents. It was the *way* I lost them."

Something in his words or expression or maybe his tone must have gotten through to her. Her eyes narrowed in curiosity and segued into concern.

She eased back onto the chair.

"Didn't they die in a car accident like my parents?"

He shook his head, barely taking time to consider the wisdom of his next words. "If I tell you something important, about me and this ranch and my parents' deaths, can you keep a secret?"

"Of course." She rolled those green irises toward the ceiling. "What do you take me for? The town crier?"

"I'm serious, Monroe. No sass, no sarcasm."

She softened. "Okay."

"I'm trusting you with the most important thing I know. The most crucial moment in my life to this point."

"You look so serious. You're starting to freak me out."

He tried for a smile, but it fell short. His insides

churned. He'd never said the words out loud to anyone but Carter, and then only the rudiments.

But he needed Monroe's assistance. She knew the area, the people. They'd be more likely to open up to her when they might not even talk to a stranger like him.

To be honest, he needed more than an employee. He needed a friend. Talking to Carter on the phone was good, but having Monroe next to him was…different. Better in a way he didn't examine.

Sliding his hand across the table, Nathan grasped the top of hers and held on. Again. Not in a romantic way. But as one desperate for human touch.

His stomach tightened. He cleared his throat. "I inherited Persimmon Hill."

She blinked. "What? I don't understand."

He sucked in a whiff of the room's leather-and-fresh-paint scent, steadied the thrumming of his pulse and held a little tighter to Monroe's fingers.

"Paul and Lisa Vandiver, the couple who died here, were my parents. I was the little boy who found them."

Chapter Six

Shock reverberated through Monroe with the force of 220 volts.

"Nathan." Her free hand went to her lips. "Oh, my goodness."

Even though Nathan had misled her in the beginning, making her believe he'd purchased the property, Monroe couldn't be angry. She understood the desperate need for privacy, the fear of prying eyes, gossip and pity.

"*You* found them?" she whispered.

She saw his Adam's apple convulse. Heard him swallow. "Yes. In the media room."

He closed his eyes, his face a study in tragedy.

What he must be feeling, remembering was almost unthinkable.

And she'd thought of him as a rich boy whose life had been easy.

"The room you keep locked?"

He nodded.

Her heart broke for him and for the six-year-old child whose life had changed in an instant. The way hers had changed at age ten. Only worse. Much, much more tragic.

Monroe flipped her palm upright and laced her fingers with his, squeezing gently as if to absorb some of his grief.

Nothing she could say or do would mend such a tragic past. Only God could do that. Her natural inclination was to battle the blaze, to take action, to heal the wound.

"I cannot imagine. I have no words."

"Now you see why everything about restoring Persimmon Hill is important to me."

"You want to give them back their dignity."

His blue eyes found hers and held, full of gratitude that she understood. "More than giving them back their dignity and reputation, Monroe, I have to know what happened and why."

"But the police surely investigated. Wasn't their report conclusive?"

"Not to me. What they claim happened doesn't fit with my memories of Mother and Dad." He told her of growing up in a loving home with a couple who doted on each other. A perfect life for a happy child. "I've never seen the actual police report, but from what I've read in old newspaper accounts, no motive was ever discovered." He pressed his lips into a tight line. "Who shoots his wife and turns the gun on himself without a good reason?"

She could not begin to fathom. Nor could she fathom the mental anguish Nathan had endured. Still did.

She didn't respond with the obvious, that as a child, his view of his parents was likely skewed and his memories doubtless limited. He needed to do this research, and who was she to disagree?

"In a way, this house does haunt you," she said. "Emotionally, anyway."

"That's why I'm compelled to talk to people who knew my parents. I need to know if my memory is reliable, or if someone knows things about my parents that I wouldn't."

The latter was a very good possibility. "You were only six."

His eyes captured hers, pleading. "So, will you go with me today?"

What else could she say?

"Yes." And so he wouldn't feel her pity, she added, "But you're buying lunch."

Monroe was a nervous wreck. Since coming home after the fire accident, she avoided public places as much as possible. The stares were too much. She'd even stopped going to church, a behavior that caused her grandfather considerable concern. But she could only handle so many sympathetic platitudes like, "you poor thing" and "bless your heart."

Life forced her into the open on occasion, but work on her family's ranch and rehabbing stray dogs gave her an excuse to stay home. She visited with a friend or two and made grocery and farm store runs where people had grown accustomed to her appearance, then hurried back home to privacy.

Home had been her refuge. Until Nathan Garrison came along with his charm and his sad story.

She was a sucker for a sad story. Just ask her dogs.

Now, she'd promised to put herself on display to introduce Nathan to people she either avoided or didn't know well.

It was a recipe for disaster. Or at least, humiliation.

She dawdled with the horses, stalling lunch until she was certain the noon rush hour at the Bea Sweet had passed.

If Nathan noticed, he went about his business with the construction and said nothing.

By the time they reached her hometown and the Bea Sweet Bakery on Main Street, only two tables were occupied.

That much was a blessing. It was hard enough to face individuals without a crowd of people staring and whispering.

"What should we order?" Nathan held her chair

and, appearing far more comfortable than she felt, scanned the old-fashioned chalkboard menu with interest.

"Pick what you like. Everything's good."

Ms. Bea, the aging bakery owner and Poppy's lady friend, came slowly from the kitchen to the front counter. "How you folks doing? Why, Monroe, is that you, honey?"

"Yes, Ms. Bea." Ms. Bea was kindness personified but the habit of averting her face was ingrained in Monroe.

"And who is this handsome cowboy with you?"

Monroe introduced Nathan, who turned on his movie-star charm. If the man could bottle that, he'd make gazillions. Interestingly, he didn't appear to realize how handsome he was, and his friendliness seemed genuine.

But what did she know? She'd been fooled before by a pretty face and a magnetic smile.

An hour and a half after enjoying a ham and cheese melt with the best tortilla soup of his life, and armed with the addresses of three locals who'd known his parents, Nathan purchased several dozen doughnuts for his work crew and left the bakery full of food and optimism.

"Do you know any of these people?" he asked Monroe as he held the truck door and waited for her to settle in the passenger seat.

"Vaguely. Summer Kleinfeld used to work at

my doctor's office. The names the carpenter gave you are familiar, too."

"You were right about Ms. Bea. She's definitely in the know." He shut the door and loped around to his side.

As he slid behind the wheel, he added, "These addresses are right here in town. Who do we see first?"

She turned wide eyes on him. "Today? You want to go today?"

"Why not? We took time away from the restoration to do this. Might as well make the most of our trip." The eagerness inside him grew the longer he was at Persimmon Hill. He was compelled to keep moving for a lot of reasons he wouldn't share with Monroe.

"I can't."

"Why not?"

"I'm taking the dogs to the vet."

This was news to him. "You're on the clock. My clock."

She bristled. "I keep my own hours."

"Since when?"

"Since you said I call the shots. If that was a lie, I quit. Take me back to Persimmon Hill. I'll collect my dogs and go home."

She crossed her arms and turned toward the side window.

Nathan blinked at the back of her head in frustration, but didn't argue. Obviously, he'd touched a nerve. Again. One minute he thought they were getting along great and the next she was the ice queen hiding behind her fortress walls.

He started the truck and backed out of the parking space. With his right hand, he pushed the bakery box in her direction until it nudged her leg.

"Want a doughnut?"

Monroe turned from the window, expression quizzical. "What?"

"Your choice. Chocolate, maple, sugar, glazed or filled. Something for everyone."

"You're a strange dude, Nathan Garrison."

He smiled. "So I've been told."

"Okay. One person." She pointed a stern finger at him. "And don't think just because you buy raspberry-filled doughnuts that I capitulate that easily."

Nathan shook his head, holding back another grin. "Never would I expect Monroe Matheson to capitulate."

She sniffed at him and turned her face toward the passenger window.

Inside Nathan celebrated. Though the task he'd set before him was daunting and somewhat grim, work on the ranch progressed nicely, and today he began the journey toward understanding what had happened to Mother and Dad. And why.

And his cranky cowgirl had "capitulated" into going along for the ride.

* * *

Summer Kleinfeld, the only person on Nathan's list whom Monroe didn't mind encountering, wasn't home. Neither was Wayne Klondike.

"They may be at work, Nathan," she reminded him, "where we should be."

Though his face registered disappointment, Nathan aimed his big truck toward the last address on the list. "You said one and I'm holding you to it."

Monroe pretended boredom but inside she was two things: nervous and compassionate. The guy had a deep need to know his parents and could only accomplish that by talking to a bunch of strangers. She had a deep need to remain as far out of the public eye as possible.

What a pair.

When they arrived at the bungalow on Barta Street, a silver Honda Civic was parked in front of the garage door.

Nathan, who'd stared silently ahead on the drive, nodded toward the car. "Someone's home."

Monroe flipped down the truck's mirrored sun visor and adjusted her hair.

He parked on the street and killed the engine. "You look fine, Monroe."

She gave him a cold glance. "Easy for you to say." He wasn't a freak.

"Hey." Reaching past the doughnut boxes, Nathan squeezed the top of her hand. "Anyone who messes with you has to come through me."

Her heart nearly stopped. Her chest got all itchy and tingly. She snatched her hand from beneath his, hopped out of the truck and marched up to the front door.

Nathan followed. She pressed the doorbell and then stood to one side to let Nathan take center stage. Maybe if she remained in the background, Rebecca Sandberg would only have eyes for the handsome man.

A dark haired, fiftyish woman in yoga attire answered the door, a pink towel slung around her neck. She remained fit and pretty, someone who worked at remaining beautiful even as she aged. Monroe remembered her from around town.

Rebecca was definitely the type to stare at silvery-blue eyes and a perfect masculine face.

Instead, the woman's gaze found Monroe first. "Monroe Matheson?"

So much for remaining incognito.

Monroe tried to shrink behind Nathan. "I wasn't sure you'd remember me."

"Of course I do. Our local Strawberry Queen, how many years in a row? And queen of everything in high school. Your picture was in the newspaper more than the mayor's."

Monroe dipped her head. Her hair tumbled forward. "Long time ago."

Rebecca touched her arm. "Hon, I was real

sorry to hear about your accident. It must be awful for someone with your looks."

The woman had no idea how awful, made worse by people who didn't know when to keep quiet. Right now, Monroe wanted to turn tail and race back to the truck to hide her awful face.

Nathan stepped slightly to one side, his wide shoulder effectively coming between her and Rebecca Sandberg.

His promise ticker-taped through her head and jump-started the tingles. Again.

"Miss Sandberg, I'm Nathan Garrison. I'm restoring the Persimmon Hill Guest Ranch and was told you knew the former owners."

"Please, it's Rebecca. Miss Sandberg makes me feel old." She gave a light laugh, fluttering a flirtatious hand.

Monroe fought not to roll her eyes.

Nathan didn't respond to the flirtatious bait.

"Would you mind talking to me about them? Would that be a problem?"

"Oh, no problem at all. You're all the buzz around town." She tilted her head, carefully made-up eyes widening at the handsome man on her doorstep. "Everyone is thrilled that someone bought Persimmon Hill and wants to reopen the ranch to guests."

"Glad to hear it." His mouth tilted upward and the hallelujah chorus erupted. From the beaming smile Rebecca offered him, she heard it, too. "Mind if we come in and ask you about them?"

"Well, no, but that was a long time ago. I'm not sure I can tell you very much."

"Anything will help." Nathan turned on his charm.

Monroe fought not to gag.

Rebecca of the skinny yoga pants patted her face with the pink towel. "Then come in. I'll tell you anything I can remember."

Inside, Monroe took the chair to the left of Rebecca, out of her direct line of sight. Nathan settled across from the other woman, his sincere gaze holding her attention.

As the pair began to discuss Lisa and Paul Vandiver, Monroe might as well have been invisible. Which was perfect, as far as she cared.

Nathan had that effect on people. He listened with his entire body as if the speaker was the most interesting, delightful companion possible. He treated her the same way.

Her stomach soured. His charm extended far beyond a hired-hand cowgirl. Hadn't she warned herself about the danger of those tingly, itchy feelings?

A wiggling puppy wove around Monroe's feet, whining softly. Monroe couldn't resist. She lifted the little white Westie onto her lap and stroked the long, soft fur. The anxiety began to seep away.

As Nathan and Rebecca talked, Monroe remained quiet, hidden in her chair, petting the sweet puppy. Her own pups were back at the ranch, probably wondering where she was. She thought she'd found a good home for Goldie, which made her happy and sad all at once.

When his conversation ended, Nathan stood and extended a hand to Rebecca. "Thank you for talking to us. When Persimmon Hill is restored, you have a personal invitation to the grand re-opening barbecue."

He was hosting a grand opening barbecue?

"My pleasure, Nathan. Everyone at my golf club is eager to see what you're doing out there and to meet you." She winked. "I beat them to the punch. At least on meeting you."

"The pleasure was all mine."

As they made their way out the door, Rebecca called out, "Monroe, it was lovely to see you again."

Monroe resisted a snort, and, without turning around, lifted a hand in farewell.

Once in the truck, she leaned her head back against the seat and chuckled. With her eyes on Nathan, Rebecca had barely realized Monroe was there.

Maybe introducing him to townsfolk wouldn't be so difficult after all.

Nathan looped his left arm over the steering wheel and turned toward her. "Strawberry queen? High school queen of everything? Why didn't you tell me I was in the presence of royalty?"

She glared at him. "Don't tease."

"I'm not. I'm impressed."

"Shut up."

"Are you trying to hurt my feelings?"

"Yes."

He laughed. The goofy man laughed. She'd never met anyone who found insults and rudeness amusing. It was as if her cynicism was a facade he could see right through.

Maybe he could.

A yearning stirred in Monroe's chest. Letting down her guard was dangerous. Keeping it up was exhausting.

Nathan started the truck, his face turned toward her, eyes serious. "Thank you for going with me. Having you there helped. Truly."

She wanted to glare at him and shrug off the remark but couldn't. His comment disarmed her. He'd needed her support, wanted her at his side.

"Being there wasn't as bad as I thought."

"Good." The corners of his mouth lifted. "We'll go see the others tomorrow."

To keep him from getting overconfident, Monroe dipped her head in a hard stare and lifted her visible eyebrow as high as possible. "Maybe."

Chapter Seven

"Things are going great. The plan, as they say, is coming together."

Nathan stood in the shade of an old oak, taking a breather while he spoke to his cousin Carter on the phone.

He mopped his face with a bandanna and swigged bottled water, his body pouring sweat from an hour of gathering and hauling trash. Construction was a hot, messy business. The last few years of mostly office work had made him soft.

"Glad to hear it," Carter said. "Think you'll get the work done in time?"

"As long as we don't have many setbacks."

"Inevitable in construction. Remember not to panic when it happens. How are things looking? Send some new pics."

Carter was like a cricket, jumping from one thing to another, a multitasker. He got more done in a day than three people. Right now, he was likely answering email, updating his calendar and planning his next homeless mission event while talking to Nathan on the phone.

Nathan could sure use him on the ranch.

"Photos coming your way." Nathan aimed his cell phone at a nearby cabin where he'd been collecting broken boards, shingles and other trash. "New roof on Cabin 3. Updated windows going in next week."

He snapped the photo and pressed Send. Monroe had helped him choose the roof color. She had a good eye and he'd come to appreciate her input, even if she attached a snarky comment to every piece of advice. Her value, he'd learned, lay in far more than horsemanship. Smart, insightful, she understood what guests would want in a ranch retreat.

"Nice," Carter commented with a hum in his throat when he'd apparently received the photo. "Looks great. I may have to take you up on that invitation."

Nathan regretted the poor rural cell service. With video chat, he could have shown Carter a lot more.

"I'm counting on it, Carter. Anytime. Or just move down here and work with me on the ranch."

Carter laughed. "Yeah, we can both envision me on a horse or catching fish."

"You catch a different kind of fish."

"Me and Jesus," his cousin said, understanding

that Nathan referred to his mission outreaches, always with the hope of introducing souls to Jesus.

"You do eternal work, my man, and there are lost souls here, too. Come on down. My house is huge. Plenty of room. No need to wait for a cabin."

"Count on it. As soon as I can." A voice in the background interrupted them.

While he waited for his cousin to speak to someone else, Nathan took a long drink of water, his eyes roaming over the beautiful land.

Each of the cabins was set deep into the trees away from the hustle and bustle of the main house and barns and separated from each other by an acre or more. If not for the distant rumble of equipment, the area would be silent. Guests would come here for the privacy as well as the beautiful surroundings.

He didn't need to worry about poor cell phone service.

Even though cell phones and internet were not as ubiquitous then as they were now, Mother and Dad had seen a need for busy people to get away to nature and refresh, to leave stress behind and renew themselves in God's majestic creation.

That would be his marketing focus. Forget cell phones and enjoy nature.

With the rumble of Carter and someone talking in the background, Nathan drew in a long, appreciative breath. For his parents who'd left him such a magnificent gift and for his Lord, Who had created a world of majestic beauty in the first place.

He could not let any of them down. People *needed* Persimmon Hill as much as he did.

"Nathan?" Carter's voice came back on the line. "You still there?"

"Still here. Man, it's hot today."

"July usually is."

July. The date tightened Nathan's gut. Mid-September was his deadline. Two and a half months and still so much to do.

"Nathan?"

"Sorry, my mind wandered."

"I get that. Crazy that you're even down there. Any repercussions of living in the house? How's that going? You okay?"

"Completely. Just wildly busy. It feels right, though, to be back at Persimmon Hill, living in the house. I almost expect to hear Mother playing the piano or to run into Dad talking to a ranch hand in one of the barns. I found a photo of the three of us in the library. We looked happy."

He realized, of course, that looks could be deceiving and photos rarely told the reality behind the smiles. Still, seeing himself bracketed on either side by his handsome parents filled a void inside him.

"Speaking of your folks," Carter said, "how's the search going?"

"So-so. Monroe has introduced me to a few

people who knew others who were acquainted with Mother and Dad, so I'm making phone calls and visits whenever I get a break from the job site." Which wasn't nearly often enough, but the ranch had to be his focus for his now.

"Are you learning anything useful?"

"So far everyone has described them the way I remember. Nice people who seemed devoted to each other. And me."

"Maybe they only say that because you're their son."

Leave it to Carter to shoot straight. He had that in common with Monroe.

"They don't know. No one except Monroe. I'm not telling anyone else for that exact reason."

"Good plan. Do any of your folks' friends have an opinion on what happened between them?"

Nathan winced. Any discussion of his parents inevitably returned to that one horrific incident. He desperately wanted to change that mindset.

"They expressed shock that a seemingly happy, successful couple with everything to live for and no obvious problems would die that way."

He refused to say murder-suicide, and wouldn't until he had no other choice.

"Even if you don't learn anything definitive about their deaths, you'll have that."

True. But he wanted more. He *needed* to understand why they died. This vast, empty, aching hole inside him would never heal until he knew.

Pivoting from the uncomfortable subject, he asked, "How's everything with you? The mission, the job? Anything interesting I need to know about?"

"Mission work is great. A couple of people accepted Jesus last week."

"Sweet."

"It's what I live for. Bringing glory to Jesus and hope to people."

That was Carter in a nutshell. He loved Jesus and people and spent every free moment trying to bring the two together. Good man, his cousin.

"How's work?"

"Summer rush as always. And dude, have you talked to Jack recently?" Jack was their boss in the busy management company where both Nathan and Carter handled construction contracts and accounts. "There are rumblings."

Frowning, Nathan pushed off the rough-barked tree. "What kind of rumblings?"

"A few coworkers are unhappy about you taking a leave of absence during the busy time of year. They're complaining about carrying your account load."

"What about the bosses?"

"Nothing there that I've heard."

Nathan was relieved but knew better than to relax much. Jack hadn't been overeager to give him this leave of absence. A few weeks was no problem but six months stretched the boss's indulgence. He'd wanted Nathan to work remotely and continue handling his construction projects, but Nathan had refused. Persimmon Hill and his search for truth required his full focus.

"Keep your ear to the ground for me, okay? I don't want to lose my seniority."

"Got it, cuz. You hang in there. Gotta get back to the grindstone."

"Me, too."

They disconnected. Nathan pocketed his phone and stared out over the vast landscape where construction moved forward at a slow, but steady, pace.

Later, he'd call Jack, make sure everything was okay with his leave. Going six months without a paycheck was hard enough. If he failed to revive Persimmon Hill in that time frame, he'd need to return to his old job and start making a living.

If the job still waited for him.

As long as nothing went wrong on Persimmon Hill, he thought he'd reach his goal and the rest would fall into place.

He'd prayed about this move and was pretty sure he'd received the green light from God—unless his personal desire had overridden his spiritual discernment. He was only an ordinary Christian man, doing the best he could, not a prophet.

Yet, the Lord had carried him throughout his life even though he hadn't noticed the tender guiding hand of Jesus until he'd accepted Him into his heart as a teenager. Then, he'd seen. Then, he'd comprehended. God had preserved his life that horrible night and given him a Christian upbringing with grandparents who, while secretive, had his best interests at heart.

Why his parents and not him?

"Mr. Garrison. Mr. Garrison!" Someone shouted his name. At the same moment his cell phone jangled.

Nathan answered. On the other end, the foreman's frantic voice filled him in on the trouble. He broke into a jog.

He was halfway across the wide expanse of green grass leading to the swimming pool when Monroe rode up beside him on a dappled gray horse. Easily handling the big animal, she held the reins in one hand and shifted in the saddle.

"I heard the commotion. What's happened?"

"An accident at the pool site." So much for nothing going wrong.

"Anyone hurt?"

"Don't know yet."

She patted the back of the saddle. "Get on. Let's go."

Admittedly, he was winded, but the idea of riding double with Monroe set up all kinds of crazy emotions in his chest.

He shook them off. At the moment, this unexpected, ongoing attraction to his testy neighbor was the least of his concerns.

Like a trick rider who'd jumped on horseback hundreds of times, he grabbed her extended arm, stuck his work boot into the stirrup and leaped onto the saddle behind her.

"Hold on," she said, but before he could, she nudged Tex into a lope.

The force jolted him backward. He grabbed for the cantle.

"I said hold on!" Monroe's sharp tone brooked no argument as she reached back and grabbed one of his wrists and yanked him against her.

He wrapped his arms around her narrow waist. She placed a hand over his and kicked the horse into high gear.

As concerned as he was to know what had happened on the construction site, Nathan's thoughts centered on the woman riding the wind in the direction of the swimming pool.

The breeze whipped her soft hair against his face, stirring the scents of lemony shampoo and fresh air.

Hot and sweaty, he probably smelled like the south end of this horse. She smelled good, like spice and leather.

Touching her was even better.

A swirl of dust struck him in the face, a slap to turn his mind away from senseless attraction and toward the gaping chasm where the pool would be and whatever disaster awaited.

Monroe would throat-punch him if she could read his wayward thoughts.

She reined Tex to a sudden stop, which pitched Nathan forward against her straight back. If he'd had a single errant thought left, she'd just knocked it out of him. Monroe released her grip on his hand.

Pulse banging in his temples for more reasons than one, Nathan slid to the ground and rushed toward a gaggle of men on the south end of the deep excavated hole.

Monroe caught up with him, boots thudding the hard-packed summer earth. No surprise. She was fast on her feet. On a horse, too, though she'd left the gray tied twenty yards away.

He had the random thought that she must have been a barrel racer at some point to ride so fast and stop so quickly.

"What's happened?" Tugging her hat low, she dipped her head and swung the side-parted hair over her scars.

Every time she did that, he wanted to hug her close and promise to protect her from any and all stares. Interesting to feel so protective about a strong woman who could obviously take care of herself.

Yet, everybody needed somebody. He certainly did.

"An excavated wall of dirt collapsed," he answered.

The collapse didn't sound serious but it was. A massive wall of dirt could cover and smother a man fast.

Rough-in plumbers and concrete framers were on site today to prepare the deep walls and bottom of the massive swimming pool for concrete. He prayed none of them were in the pit when the wall caved in.

He and Monroe hurried around the piles of equipment toward a skid steer now stuck at an awkward angle down a collapsing incline. Plumbing supplies the machine had been moving lay jumbled at the bottom of the ten-foot hole.

A crowd of workmen in hard hats surrounded the pit, voices high with tension. Although living in Houston meant Nathan knew a rudiment of Spanish, their rapid-fire excitement was too much for him.

To a man they stared down inside the vast dig.

Nathan strained toward the excavated site. Supplies could be replaced. People couldn't.

"Anyone still down there?" Nathan called.

Dirt from the edges of the excavation had been dislodged, collapsing one wall where the machine had been working. A wide river of dirt continued to slide precariously downward, shifting the side-tilted machine inch by inch.

Nathan's breath stuck in his throat.

Joseph, the operator, eyes wide with fear, remained inside the skid steer.

"Get back," Nathan yelled to the crowd, his arms waving every onlooker away from the yawning abyss. "Everyone move back before this thing collapses and we all go down."

Another spattering of Spanish rose in the air. This he understood.

In a calm, authoritative voice, he focused on the operator. He was thankful the man was physically fit and young enough to do what must be done.

"Joseph, when I give the signal, jump as far to the right, away from the machine as you can. Forget the skid steer. Just get out safely. We've got you."

More dirt cascaded into the massive hole.

Joseph nodded his understanding.

"Eddie, Tim, you and some of you other men be ready to drag him clear. Manuel, find a rope. Quick. Pablo, ready the shovels just in case."

He hoped they wouldn't need the last two but was taking no chances on a man being buried alive. He'd seen it happen. Heavy soil could crush a man to death in minutes.

Chattering in Spanish, shouting orders to one another, the men scrambled to do his bidding.

While Nathan held his breath and prayed amid a smattering of other voices praying aloud, Joseph crossed himself and leaped free of the machine. He fell, rose, then began a mad, clawing scramble up the steep incline.

The sudden motion rocked the big machine. Heavy waves of soil tumbled inward in an avalanche. Joseph struggled against the mounds already encasing his feet and ankles.

He fell to his knees.

"God help him." He'd no more than said the words than Tim and Eddie, in an act of bravery bordering on stupidity, slid down the embankment toward their fallen friend.

Joseph pushed to his feet again and fought his way to the hands extended to pull him to safety.

Giving a wide berth to the collapsing wall, Nathan circled around to the men. Joseph lay on the bare ground, breathless.

"You okay? How's your leg? Do you need an ambulance? Let's get you to the ER."

He yanked his phone out, ready to call 9-1-1.

Joseph waved both hands, stirring the dust from his covered arms and shirt.

"All okay, boss." The man's accent thickened. "Gracias." He crossed himself and muttered a Spanish thanks.

Three more of Joseph's coworkers came up beside them. "The wall collapsed on its own, Mr. Garrison. Joseph did nothing wrong."

These men, mostly immigrants, constantly worried about losing their jobs. They worked hard and fast from sunrise to sunset, barely taking the breaks he required of them. He valued them and

their work ethic, though getting them to understand his appreciation would require proof.

"Accidents happen. I just don't want anyone
hurt. Understand? We do this safely or not at all.
Nothing is worth your life."

"Si. Si." Joseph patted himself down and
dusted his knees. "No hurt."

Monroe, who'd trailed Nathan to this side of
the excavation, stepped close to the operator. "Are
you sure? You took a tumble when you jumped. I
saw your knee give way. We should check it out.
Understand?"

Though her hair and hat covered the left side of
her face, she didn't seem concerned about being
noticed at the moment. Her focus was on the slender, possibly injured Mexican.

Nathan loved seeing this side of her. Tough
girl cared.

Joseph gazed down at his dirt-covered pants.
"No, no. No *estoy herido*. Is okay, senorita. Gracias, gracias."

Monroe nodded and spun toward the still-col-
lapsing wall and echoed Nathan's worry. "Was
anyone down there when the avalanche started?"

A broad-chested plumber, tool belt dragging
his pants low, raised his hand. "I was, but I got
out quick." He laughed and patted his paunch. "I
move pretty fast for a fat man."

Though the men chuckled and tried to lighten
the mood by slapping the plumber and Joseph

on the back and making jokes, Nathan's insides rattled. This could have been a disaster.

Thank You, God, that no one was seriously injured.

"Joseph, take the rest of the afternoon off with pay. You guys working the pit grab a break while Eddie and I figure out what to do about this."

Nodding and talking, the men did as he asked while the on-looking crowd of workmen dispersed back to their assigned tasks.

Nathan was certain he heard Joseph laugh.

He'd probably be back on the job in thirty minutes.

Shaking his head at the resilience of his construction crew, he stacked his hands on his hips and surveyed the skid steer now on its side and the massive wall of dirt that continued to slide downward.

"Can we stabilize that wall enough to get the machinery out safely?"

"I can pull it out with Tex," Monroe said.

Nathan gave her a sideways glance. "Too dangerous. We'll get a crane in here."

"Costly solution when I can do it for free."

Adrenaline still pumped through his veins at the speed of sound.

The idea of Monroe risking herself and an animal ripped through him. No way. No stinkin' way.

She was too important.

"I said no, Monroe. And that's the end of the conversation." His tone, he realized, was sharp and terse.

Her offended expression said she didn't like it one bit.

She stared at him for two beats, lips tight, then spun on her boot heel and stormed away.

The crew foreman, Eddie, slapped him on the shoulder. "Your woman isn't too happy with you."

"She's not my woman." He liked her, enjoyed their verbal spars, thought she was beautiful and interesting. She'd become important to him.

But she was not his woman.

The denial settled on his stomach along with a heavy dose of acid.

Even if he wanted Monroe to be more than an employee, he'd probably made her angry enough just now to quit.

"Take five. I'll be back."

He executed a one-eighty in the direction she'd gone. Time to mend a fence.

Eddie patted his shoulder again.

"Not your woman, huh?" And then the man laughed.

"He may be my boss, but he has no right to talk to me that way."

Inside the horse barn, Monroe fumed as she unsaddled Tex and brushed him down. Every brush stroke relieved some of her aggravation.

"I'm going to let him have it, too," she murmured. "Maybe I'll quit."

Except she couldn't. She needed this job, and more than that, she liked it. Working with the dogs and horses while watching Persimmon Hill come back to life induced a contentment she hadn't felt since before the fire.

Nathan was rarely grumpy. Mostly, he liked having her around. He asked for her ideas. Listened to her as if she had a brain. Never seemed to notice her horrendously ugly scars. Not even once.

"He shouldn't have talked to me like that in front of the other employees. Or anywhere else, for that matter." The only people she'd ever allowed to speak harshly to her were military superiors.

She wasn't in the Navy anymore. And he might be her boss, but he was not her superior.

As if in sympathy, the old gray horse nuzzled her back. He'd been a ranch horse working cattle and riding fence every day, but he liked people and was perfect for inexperienced guests. And he'd proved today he still had some juice in him.

The dogs, trained to remain around the barns and out of the way, swarmed around her feet. Tex paid them no mind.

"You're going to rub the hide off that horse."

At Nathan's voice, Monroe stiffened but didn't turn around to face him. One hand on Tex's mane, the other on the brush, she said, "If you have something to say to me, say it, don't yell it."

"Did I yell? I rarely yell."

That was true. Nathan used persuasive charm to get things done his way. He didn't have to raise his voice.

When she didn't bother to reply, he went on, "I shouldn't have snapped at you, but can you spare me some grace because of the intense situation?"

Her hands paused on the horse's muscular neck. He was right. The situation had been scary. Emotions ran high. She was only upset because he'd embarrassed her in front of the construction crew.

Grace. He'd asked for *grace*, a word that always turned her mind to Jesus and the grace He extended to anyone who'd receive it.

She had a lot of trouble accepting that gift.

With a guilty sigh, she tossed the brush into the grooming bucket and turned. "Just because I forgive you doesn't mean I like you."

A flirty little quiver played around his mouth. "Understood. Let me buy you a shrimp dinner as proof of my contrition."

Dinner? Seriously? She was upset but hadn't expected the offer of dinner as a makeup gesture.

Monroe's pulse did a silly little tap dance at the idea. Dinner, sort of like a date. Except she didn't date.

Most certainly she did not date overly handsome , uber-charming men who made her itchy.

Discomfited, she slid the bridle from Tex's head and patted his hip, pushing him toward the open door and the grass-filled pasture beyond.

"Well?" Nathan asked. "What do you say?"

In self-preservation before her heart overrode bad experience, she said, "I don't like fish."

"Technically," he said, with that little half smile that made her itchy, "shrimp is not fish."

"I still don't like it." She turned her back on him to hang the grooming bucket on a hook inside the open tack room.

A strong, masculine hand landed lightly on her left shoulder. "Hey."

Her body tensed. Beneath that hand, under the loose linen blouse, was a ripple of burn scars no one ever saw but her. Could he feel them? Would he be repulsed? "What?"

"A construction site is a dangerous place." Something in his tone had changed.

"I know that."

"You don't understand. I don't want people hurt." He gently tugged until she pivoted to face him. "I don't want *you* hurt, Monroe."

All the tingles and itchiness available on planet Earth set up shop in Monroe's chest.

What was he saying? That she mattered to him?

"I do understand," she said in self-defense. "Injured workmen cause delays and cost money. Stop fretting. I promise not to sue you if I get hurt."

That flirty little lip quiver flatlined. His other hand came down on her opposite shoulder, holding her at half an arm's length.

Too close, yet not close enough.

A throb pulsed against the inside of her rib cage.

Drat. Oh, drat, and kick a door. She liked the guy too much.

Every cell in her body yearned toward him, toward his kindness, his genuine decency, his strength.

She'd never needed anyone's strength. She had her own.

His eyes, those fascinating silvery-blue orbs, looked at her with a tenderness that made her throat ache.

And her chest itch.

He shook his head, the little smile returning to his mouth. Oh, that handsome mouth. "Stubborn, stubborn woman. What shall I do with you."

His hands slid down her arms, floating over her long, scar-covering sleeves to grasp her hands. His were hard and calloused from the weeks of work. Masculine in a way that made her throat thicken.

He gave a gentle tug, urging her closer but giving her the option of staying right where she was.

She didn't need him. Didn't need anyone but her horses and dogs.

Yet, Monroe took those two steps and found herself in the circle of Nathan's arms.

He titled his head, a soft smile playing around the corners of his lips.

Had the man lost his senses?

Was he about to kiss her? *Her?* The ugly duckling?

Maybe she was the one who'd lost her senses.

She, who'd never planned to let another man anywhere near her, wanted to kiss the handsome prince.

Monroe had the random, ridiculous thought that if he kissed her, maybe she'd no longer be a frog.

Heart thundering, she leaned in.

Suddenly, Peabody, the pit bull with no manners at all, rammed his enormous body in between them, whining like a pouty baby.

Monroe jerked away from Nathan, both relieved and disappointed at the interruption.

Going to her haunches, she buried her blazing face in the dog's neck. Something had scared the big sissy. A noise, a flapping bird, another dog, anything. Even a blowing piece of paper. He was such a scaredy-cat. Like her.

Scared of life because of the scars they carried.

The ache in her heart throbbed relentlessly. A weaker woman would have cried.

In the distance, construction noise rumbled on, but silence fell between Monroe and Nathan. What could she say? She'd almost made a fool of herself.

Nathan pitied her. That's all his attentions and insistence could be. No man with his looks, charm and money could find a woman like her attractive.

"Guess I'll get back to work unless—" Nathan seemed to hesitate.

She nodded, wanting him to stay, longing for him to hold her, kiss her, *care* about her, but painfully aware that God didn't answer those kinds of prayers. She knew because she'd prayed them before. Tony had broken off their relationship anyway.

With one hand on Peabody's head, she rose to her feet. She couldn't even think of a snarky comment. "Me, too."

For another long moment, Nathan remained in the barn breezeway, gilded by sunlight, looking dirty and sweaty and incredibly appealing while she mentally kicked herself.

He started to turn away and then pivoted back to point at her. "Pick your favorite meal. I owe you dinner, and Nathan Garrison pays his debts."

Chapter Eight

The collapsed wall hadn't been disastrous, thankfully. But the delay had set them back two days. Add to that the interesting tension between him and Monroe, and Nathan hadn't slept much the last couple of nights.

He was attracted to her. He'd already acknowledged that.

Though she'd fussed about the promised dinner in her usual sarcastic manner, she'd finally agreed to it as long as the meal was on her terms.

He still didn't know what those terms were, which made him jittery in a good way. He hadn't been out with a woman he truly liked in three years, even if Monroe did insist that theirs was not a date. It was, she claimed, a payback meal. An apology for barking at her in front of the men.

Whatever. Nathan looked forward to spending time with the sassy cowgirl that didn't involve work or a pack of dogs that had terrible timing.

He would have kissed her if not for Peabody. Would she have slugged him?

He didn't think so. Without being overconfident, he had the sneaking feeling that behind that protective wall, Monroe liked him, too.

His cell phone rang. Hoping it was Monroe with the directions to their mystery meal, he answered.

"Nathan." The person on the other end was female, but she was not Monroe.

"Grandmother." His shoulders tensed. He squeezed the tightening muscle at the base of his neck. "How are you?"

"Grandpa and I are fine. We're worried about you."

"No need. I'm good. The restoration is coming along well." Not perfectly, and he was starting to feel the time crunch. Grandmother did not need to know that.

If he said a word to her about the delays, she'd pressure him to sell out and forget the place. Again.

"About the ranch, honey. How are you balancing that and your job? Can you afford to ignore your career? I can't fathom why you insist on digging up old memories that can only hurt you."

"We've been over this before, Grandmother."

She sighed. "I know, Nathan, but honey, Granddad and I don't want you to suffer any more than you already have. Sell that awful place, take the money and buy a nice home without ugly memories and settle down here in Houston. We miss you."

There it was. The pressure he'd suspected was coming the moment he heard her voice.

His insides knotted every time they had this conversation. His grandparents desired to protect him. They wanted him to forget the past, but he couldn't. As much as he respected them and their advice, selling Persimmon Hill would be like selling a piece of his heart. He couldn't do it, not now that he was here and had experienced the deep satisfaction of coming home again.

"Understood. I love you, Grandmother." He glanced at his watch. "Sorry to rush, but I'm about to go out to dinner. Tell Grandpa I love him, too."

"Dinner? As in a date?" Before he could confirm or deny, his grandmother jumped to the conclusion she wanted. "That's marvelous, son. After Clare, you deserve to find a nice woman. Is she a Christian? I imagine she's beautiful."

Although Monroe insisted their meal was not a date, maybe it was to him.

"Yes, to both."

"Oh, this is such good news." Her tone, solemn and worried a moment before, now sounded lighter. "You go on and have fun. Forget about that terrible place and come home soon. We love you."

"Bye now." Nathan quietly ended the call, pondering his grandparents' insistent attitude that Persimmon Hill was somehow an evil place.

Pocketing the phone, he went to stand in front of the mirror on the upstairs landing. As he checked out his appearance, he was once more reminded of his mother doing the same when he was a boy.

He'd chosen a blue button-down shirt, which supposedly made his eyes bluer. Mother had often worn blue, too, for the same reason. Though Nathan wasn't much given to such vanity, tonight he wanted to look nice. His cowboy-cut jeans were newer, boots polished, and he'd added a wide belt buckle. He could imagine Monroe wrinkling her nose when she saw it.

He actually looked forward to the moment she called him a drugstore cowboy.

Humming, he bounded down the stairs and out the door where his truck was still parked from several trips into town for supplies of one kind or the other.

As he opened the door, he paused to listen. Construction sounds had ceased for the day.

The country quiet was broken only by the hum of tree frogs and cicadas and occasional bird twitter. Peaceful. Beautiful.

A giant fire-orange sun dangled above the horizon, slicing over the low mountains and through the hillside trees in stunning rays.

Guests would love coming here to escape the frantic rush of daily life.

He loved being here.

He'd come to understand why Monroe called Persimmon Hill her sanctuary. Surprisingly, unexpectedly, it had become the same for him.

He wanted it to be that for his guests, as well.

Satisfaction settled over him. Even with the work delays and added pressure from his grandparents and his other job, this was where he wanted to be.

God had guided him back to Persimmon Hill for a reason. He was sure of it now, as he hadn't been at first. Whether that reason was information about his parents or the satisfaction of restoring the guest ranch, God was in this place.

Gratitude engulfed Nathan. "Thank you, Father God."

Taking in a deep draught of clean air, Nathan climbed inside the truck and headed to Monroe's home.

Turning the radio from his usual country station to Christian music, he prayed and praised his way over the gravel and dirt roads.

Once at Monroe's door, he knocked, but before she could answer, her dogs spotted him and came running, tails in hyper-speed.

He held his hand out flat the way he'd seen Monroe do. "Sit. No jumping. I'm spiffed up for a date."

Five dogs immediately plopped on their bottoms on the wooden porch.

Nathan patted each head.

"You." He pointed at Peabody. "I'm not too happy with you, bud. You interrupted something important the other day, and I have a long memory."

The pit tilted his head to one side, his scarred ear perked in curiosity.

"Don't play innocent. You know what you did. Don't do it again."

Peabody thumped his tail and smiled as Nathan moved down the line of dogs, leaving no one out.

He wasn't really mad at Peabody, but the dog sure had bad timing.

Nathan had wanted to kiss Monroe. Still did, just as he wanted to break through that invisible shield she'd erected. She brought out his protective, fixer side.

When he came to the diminutive Rake, Nathan crouched on his boot toes to pick leaves from the tangled coat.

The front door opened and a pair of turquoise-and-brown boots appeared in his line of vision.

"I brushed him out not an hour ago."

Nathan glanced up…and lost his breath. Monroe had "spiffed up," too. He'd never seen her in a dress.

Tonight she wore a loose white sundress under a lightweight denim jacket. Like his, her boots were polished to a sheen. Around her neck, and vivid against the white dress, was a squash-blossom necklace and several additional strands of turquoise jewelry.

She'd added red lipstick and swooped her hair in a thick wave over one eye. The other side of her hair hooked behind one ear. A silver feather earring flashed in the sunlight.

Nathan swallowed hard and reminded his eyeballs to get back in his head.

Monroe Matheson was the most beautiful woman he'd ever seen. All cowgirl. All woman.

He cleared his throat, finally found his voice and asked the first thing that came to him.

Indicating Rake, he said, "Why not have him groomed and cut all that tangled fur off?"

"My dogs live outside. He'd be more uncomfortable without fur. For him, it would be like me shaving my head."

"Ah. Don't do that." Holding his overpriced Stetson, bought to impress the loan company, against one knee, Nathan pushed to a stand.

Now that he'd found his tongue and gotten his heart rate down to Mach speed, he couldn't help commenting on her outfit. "You look amazing. We must be going somewhere special."

"Count on it. Special to me, for sure." She held the screen door open. "Come on in."

Nathan bent to give the adoring Rake one last pat before trailing her into the house.

* * *

Monroe was nervous. Would Nathan approve? Or be disappointed?

She didn't want him to be disappointed.

All afternoon, she'd been jittery as a cat in a room full of rocking chairs, which was ridiculous. She couldn't care less whether Nathan Garrison liked her or not. Except she did care, and caring scared her.

"You don't look too bad yourself." She searched for a reason to poke fun at him but found nothing. He was knock-your-hat-in-the-dirt handsome, as usual, although he'd stepped up his game from casual business or grubby construction worker to Western attire that really appealed to the cowgirl in her.

"Thanks."

Before he could get a big head, she added, "For a rhinestone cowboy." She sniffed. "Greenhorn. Look at that belt buckle."

Instead of being insulted, Nathan laughed. "I was waiting for that."

"You enjoy being insulted?"

"By you." He winked. "Because I know you don't mean it. Insults are your love language."

That was the problem with Nathan. Or one of them. He seemed to look right past her attitude to the defensive posture behind it. "I don't have a love language."

"Sure you do." He glanced around the empty

living room. Poppy was visiting Ms. Bea. Harlow and family had gone back to Florida. "So where are we having this non-date dinner?"

"By the creek. I packed a picnic. Fried chicken." For the tenth time, Monroe second-guessed dressing up tonight. She didn't know why she'd felt compelled to look her best. No amount of jewelry or makeup could cover the scars. She'd never feel pretty again, not like she once had.

Would Nathan get the wrong idea?

While she wrestled self-doubts, Nathan stared at her. His stares made her uncomfortable.

"I love fried chicken," he said, "but I'm supposed to be buying dinner for you, not the other way around."

"You said I could choose. I chose a picnic at the creek." Which made wearing a dress seem all the sillier. Maybe she should change.

"I see." He studied her again. She squirmed under his appraisal. "Monroe—"

Confident he was about to discuss her ugly scars, she interrupted him. "Please, don't."

He raised both hands in surrender. "Your wish is my command."

If only all wishes were so easily granted. Or that prayers for restoration got answered. They didn't. She had to learn to live with what life had handed her.

With Nathan following, she led the way through the living room and into the kitchen where a picnic basket awaited, acutely aware of her boss's hand at the small of her back. Polite. Courteous. Touchy-feely in a positive, respectful manner.

Nathan Garrison, rhinestone cowboy, boss and neighbor, took her breath away. Not his looks in particular, although those were considerable, but him, the hardworking, determined man who exuded kindness and courtesy. With his horrific past, he could have been bitter and angry, but he'd battled past the negative to become a decent man.

As much as Monroe fought the emotion, she was falling for him.

Foolish, stupid. A sure path to more heartbreak.

She shouldn't have dressed up tonight. He'd get the wrong idea. Or was it the right one?

She was so confused at times, she wanted to run away.

She whirled around. "I'm going to change into jeans."

His silvery eyes slid over her, warm and appreciative. "Don't do that. You're always beautiful, but tonight. Wow." He patted a hand over his heart.

What was he saying? That he found her attractive? Or was he showering her with pity.

Fidgety, off-balance, she rubbed her lips together before saying, "Maybe we should eat here and forget the rest. Call it good."

"Not a chance. You are not backing out on me, Monroe. If I hadn't agreed to let you choose, I'd insist we drive to The Rooftop and order something outrageous and delicious." He lifted an eyebrow, teasing. "Like shrimp."

Good. They were back on snarky ground. She wrinkled her nose. "Bottom-feeders."

"So is it scavenger shrimp on The Rooftop or private picnic at the creek? Your choice."

Struggling to regain her internal footing, Monroe rolled her eyes. "You are such a brat."

Before she could grab the picnic basket and flounce out the door in a pretend huff, Nathan hooked a muscled forearm through the handle, strode to the back door and opened it for her.

"Thank you," she murmured, discomfited by his insistence on courtly manners and his comment that she was always beautiful. Really? The man had her head in a spin. She was an independent woman who could open doors for herself, but my goodness, Nathan made her feel special.

And she loved the way he teased, giving as good as he got. And she made sure he got plenty.

She sniffed. "Pretty nice manners for a greenhorn."

"Walking or driving?"

"Riding. The horse is ready and waiting."

She shot him a glance. His surprised expression tickled her.

"Horse? As in one single horse? But you're wearing a dress."

Monroe dipped a curtsy. "My, how observant you are. You're the one who told me not to change."

Wanting to keep the surprise as long as possible, she didn't explain, but led him through the breezeway of the barn.

As they exited the barn into the corral, Nathan sucked in an audible breath and whirled toward her. "You're kidding me?"

Second guesses crowded into Monroe's head, but she was not about to let Nathan see her uncertainty. This was probably a silly idea. "What do you think?"

While her pulse rat-a-tatted and her stomach quivered, Nathan stared at the black Morgan horse and the small open carriage waiting in the corral.

"This is awesome. Where did you get it? I want one for Persimmon Hill."

Okay. Now, she felt better. "Poppy bought it at an Amish auction, mostly to drive in parades now that he doesn't ride as much as he once did. But we use it around the ranch some too, and my nephew begs to go for rides."

"Do you know how to drive it?"

Monroe aimed one of her iciest glares at him and arched an eyebrow. "Why don't you get in, cowboy, and find out?"

* * *

Nathan had thought Monroe was interesting before, but this took things to a whole new level.

A horse and carriage? A sunset picnic? If Monroe wasn't jabbing him constantly with her barbs, he'd think the cowgirl had a romantic streak.

And if she did, he was going to enjoy it to the fullest.

Stepping to the carriage, he extended a hand in his most courtly imitation of a European prince. "Your carriage awaits, beautiful lady."

As if she suspected a joke, she stared at him, head tilted, eyes squinted for three long beats before succumbing to his manners. She placed her fingers in his and let him steady her as she took the first step and then settled into the driver's seat.

He wasn't joking about anything.

Going around to the passenger side, he climbed aboard. Monroe gently shook the reins and they were off, the big Morgan easily pulling them along the cow trails and across the pasture.

"I thought you might laugh."

"Only with delight."

Monroe's head turned toward him. "Really? You don't think I'm ridiculous for choosing this?"

"Not even close."

He thought she was afraid of going out in public. He thought she was beautiful, fascinating and challenging. He did not think she was ridiculous.

"This is fun. Unique. It gives me all kinds of ideas for the guest ranch."

"Me, too." She sat stiff and straight, keeping her head slightly turned to block his view of her left side.

The action made his heart hurt.

The last thing he wanted was for Monroe to believe she had to hide from him. At Persimmon Hill, she didn't bother. But tonight, she'd reverted, as if she knew this was a date but feared rejection.

In his mind, this was definitely a date, taken to new heights when he'd helped her into this carriage and whiffed the enchanting scent of her exotic spice.

"You don't have to be anxious with me, Monroe."

She stared straight ahead. "Why would you think I'm anxious?"

He smiled sadly and shook his head.

Using the kind of friendly small talk that worked well in his contracting business, Nathan drew her out, asking her opinion on other areas of the guest remodel, segueing to promotion and the new website, townspeople he'd met, their ongoing search for information about his parents. He told her about growing up in Houston. After a bit, she relaxed and shared about her childhood with two sisters and her grandfather.

They came to a path that led over a pond dam and ran alongside a wide, flowing creek.

As though familiar with the journey, the horse followed the scenic path, past striated rock formations and towering pines. Weeping willows dangled feathery green branches into the creek where tadpoles darted over the rocks.

Monroe pointed. "Up ahead. See the firepit?"

He did. Forty feet from the creek bank, in a circular clearing surrounded by trees, someone had created a firepit from native rock.

"Did you do this?"

"My sisters and I, years ago, but recently, Nash and Harlow cleaned it up, dug down deeper and made it better. Safer for my nephew. We do hot dogs and s'mores down here pretty often."

"And wade in the creek?"

"Of course. Davis, my nephew, especially, but we girls get in on the act, too. Chasing tadpoles." Voice nostalgic, a soft smile tugged at the corner of her mouth. "We played down here a lot as kids. Nash, Harlow's husband, who was our neighbor back then, played here with us. Poor guy. All us girls ganged up on the lone male. He was an only child and probably only put up with us in order to have someone to play with."

Nathan could see that. Monroe splashing everyone, squealing, laughing. She needed to laugh more.

He made a promise to himself to give her more reasons to laugh.

A twinge of warning pinged at him. Getting

romantically involved with Monroe was not wise. He was too busy. She had too many walls around her. They'd both lost at love before.

He still wanted to hear her laugh.

"Growing up in the city, I've never had the opportunity to hang out in the woods. Not that I recall." Had he and his parents never played in the creek behind Persimmon Hill or fished in the ponds? He couldn't remember. "Don't think I've ever chased tadpoles."

"Poor little rich kid."

There she went again. Calling him rich. What would she think if she knew he was one step away from bankruptcy?

Not her problem. Or her business. His finances, like Persimmon Hill, were his worry. The responsibility weighed on him every minute.

They came alongside the clearing where Monroe stopped the carriage. He hopped down and then helped her alight, pleased that she allowed his courtesy. Monroe needed to know he respected her as a woman and treasured her friendship. Or whatever this desire to be with her was.

As they removed the picnic basket, she asked, "What do you remember about being a little boy at Persimmon Hill?"

A vision of red flashed behind Nathan's eyes. That terrible morning. The images in the theater room.

He swallowed the painful need to be sick. The

uneasy feeling that he couldn't remember something important pushed against his rib cage, clawing for release.

"Nathan?" Monroe touched his upper arm. "Are you okay? I'm sorry if I brought up a painful memory."

A shudder ran down his spine. He shook his head, hard, and focused on the pretty clearing. Someone had set up a heavy wooden bench and rolled huge, flat rocks into a circle around the fire, along with a couple of upturned tree stumps.

Rustic. Inviting. A gathering place.

"I'm good. Sometimes the one terrible memory sneaks up on me. Mostly, I recall the good things."

"How do you remember the good when such a horrific thing happened to you?" She began to stack sticks and logs into the firepit.

Nathan spread a blanket across the weathered wooden bench and then stooped to help her.

"When I first went to live with my grandparents, I was a mess. Angry. Nightmares. Lots of trauma behaviors. I must have driven them up a wall."

He owed them so much. Even with the secrets, they'd raised him well and put up with a lot from an emotionally wounded child.

"That's sad, Nathan. I'm really sorry. No child should endure that."

"But here's the deal. Grandmother taught me

a Bible verse and read it to me every morning and night."

"What was it?"

"I can't quote it exactly but the gist is drilled into my soul. It's in Philippians and says to think on things that are lovely and of good report. Any kind of positive thing." He crouched beside the firepit. "When I would get upset about my parents, Grandmother would remind me about something I did with them that was fun. My pony. A parade. Christmas morning. Anything that would move my focus from the heartache to the joy."

"Your grandma must love you a lot."

"She does." Which made him feel guilty for going against her wishes.

Monroe topped off the campfire with one final log. "There. Ready to light when the stars come out."

His belly quivered. A campfire at night, alone in the woods with a beautiful, interesting woman, sounded romantic to him.

Did she feel the same?

"The fire doesn't bother you?" he asked, and then wanted to bite his tongue off. He'd never asked how she was burned.

His boots scraped against the hard-packed clearing as he rotated toward her. "Forget I asked. Bad topic."

"It's all right. As you said, focus on the good. I survived."

"A blessing."

She jerked one denim-clad shoulder. "Some days the jury is out on whether survival was in my best interest, but not so much lately."

His heart jumped. "Why lately?"

"I've found purpose again. Rehabbing dogs and finding them loving homes. Restoring Persimmon Hill."

Disappointment slid over him. He'd wanted her to say he was the cause of her improved happiness.

Which meant he hadn't quite pushed through her fortress walls yet.

But he wanted to. Yet, there was this push, pull between them. One step forward. One step back. Tonight, the tugs were all forward.

"Did you bring a lighter for the firepit?" Nathan crouched next to her and the neatly stacked, rust-colored rocks.

Monroe stood and dusted her hands together, drawing his eyes upward and his breath inward. So pretty. He wondered again about her choice of a white dress. Had she wanted to look pretty for him tonight?

He swallowed, his breath short in his throat, hoping so.

"Nah," she said, "I expect you to man up and rub two sticks together. Impress me with your macho prowess."

Nathan chuckled as he stood to his feet. "I can

do that. Take two matchsticks, rub the heads together and voila, fire."

Monroe snorted. "Some Boy Scout you are."

"What's in the basket?" He flipped open the lid. "Are you going to feed me or insult me?"

This time she laughed. "Both."

An hour later as they lingered over chocolate chip cookies and sweet tea, the sun had disappeared in a blaze of awe-inspiring glory and left them in the smoky twilight until stars popped out, one by one, in the sky above the creek.

Bullfrogs pulsed their foghorn songs and the steady symphony of cicadas provided background music to the water's bubble and trickle.

The conversation between her and Nathan bounced from one topic to another, easy and friendly. Even though they spent each day together at the ranch, they still found more to talk about. Monroe found that odd but comforting. Since the burn accident, the only people she cared to talk to were family.

Nathan was different.

She did not want to examine why. Tonight she simply wanted to enjoy being with someone she genuinely liked.

"So peaceful here."

Monroe appreciated darkness. At night, without light, the playing field was even. She could relax and let down her guard.

She caught the thought and turned it over in her head. With Nathan, she was relaxed most of the time, which scared her a little. He was becoming too dear to her.

Tonight had rattled her. No doubt about it.

She liked him more than a little.

Dressing up for their dinner and then seeing Nathan decked out like a rodeo cowboy pinged in all the romantic spaces inside her head. Spaces she'd tried to plug with fury and a big dose of I-don't-care. Even when she did care.

She'd been burned twice. Once by the fire and then by her fiancé. Once burned, twice warned. Twice burned and the warning took deep root. Another would turn her to ash.

"When I was a kid," she said, tilting her head back to stare upward, "Harlow and Taylor and I would lie on one of our grandma's old quilts in the front yard and watch for falling stars."

"You don't see many of those in a city."

"Certain times of the year, they're easy to spot out here away from all the lights of town. I saw a meteorite fall once."

"Yeah? How is a meteorite different from a shooting star?"

Shoulders and sides touching, the picnic basket on the ground in front, they both gazed toward the glittered sky. Monroe felt the rise and fall of Nathan's breathing, the warmth of his body through the sleeve of her jacket.

Awareness. That was the only word she could think of that fit the occasion.

Her pulse bumped in pleasant little jitters against her collarbone while a corner of her mind shouted warnings.

Angling her knees toward Nathan and her shoulders away from his tempting touch, Monroe closed her eyes, tried to ignore his masculine appeal and the scent of equally masculine cologne as she visualized the fireball.

"What I saw was close to the earth, right over the treetops, and it lasted a long time. Falling stars disappear fast." Her voice had gone soft and dreamy. She hoped he didn't think it was because of him, even though it might be.

Holding a hand toward the sky, she imitated the meteorite's arc. "A vivid ball of fire with a tail, like a comet but a rich, deep blue, streaked from one side of the dark sky to another before I lost it behind the trees. It was spectacularly beautiful. I'll never forget it."

"Reminds me of a Bible verse. Stars, moon, sun, planets. God created them all and calls them by name. Even that fireball you saw had a special name."

"Pretty cool when I think about how lucky I was to see it."

"I don't believe much in luck," he said. "You were meant to see it. Maybe God knew you needed something rare and wonderful to be reminded that He created everything in the world, including you. Everything He created is special. You're special."

Who was he kidding? The scars on her face were the only special thing about her and they weren't the kind of special anyone wanted. "I doubt that."

"I don't. You were blessed."

His frequent references to God reminded her how angry she'd been, still was, with the Almighty.

"Maybe." She'd not thought of herself as blessed in a long time, but Nathan kept reminding her.

He laced his fingers with hers and squeezed. "I wish I could have experienced the meteorite with you."

"Me, too." She swallowed, aware that her voice held a longing she tried to hide. Seeing a meteorite or even a falling star with Nathan would be memorable in a way she wasn't ready to contemplate.

She was not, however, about to suggest lying on the ground on Grandma's old quilt to stare at the sky tonight. Being alone on this non-date with Nathan was temptation enough. She certainly wasn't taking a chance on falling in love with him.

One such heartbreak was enough to last a lifetime.

And a man as handsome and charming as Nathan was sure to shred her already battered heart.

Except, tonight, she was having a hard time remembering the danger.

Confused emotions tumbling like bricks in a demolition, Monroe jerked her hand from his and began packing away the remnants of their picnic. "We should go."

She could feel his quiet gaze on her suddenly frenetic actions.

"We haven't lit the campfire yet."

"It's late."

"No, it's not. What's the real reason you want to leave? Did I say something? Are you mad because I wanted to hold your hand? Or are you worried about the fire?"

"Fire I can control doesn't scare me." The emotions running wild in her chest were the problem, not the fire.

"Okay." As mildly as if she'd not declared their need to leave, he took the lighter she'd packed from the picnic basket and crouched on his boot toes beside the rock pit. "You want to tell me about that?"

"About what?"

He flicked the lighter and in seconds the dead kindling ignited, casting Nathan's serious face in flickering shadows. "The fire."

Monroe shivered. "Not particularly."

"Okay. Want s'mores?"

Just as he'd done so many times, Nathan surprised her by veering away from any topic that made her uncomfortable. His compassion disarmed her.

"You're a nice man, Nathan Garrison. I might even like you." She didn't know why she'd admitted such a thing. She was having hard enough time thinking it.

Nathan's boots crunched as he pivoted toward her, smile gentle in the glow of the campfire. "I might like you, too."

Chapter Nine

She might like him.

Nathan smiled to himself the rest of their time at the picnic site and as they loaded the carriage and started back to her house.

He more than liked Monroe. He was falling for the prickly cowgirl. As odd as it sounded, even to him, she was easy to love. She just didn't know it yet. And he wasn't foolish enough to tell her and chance having her run away.

He wasn't ready to have his heart stomped again. With anger and pain rumbling around inside her, ready to erupt, Monroe was the kind of woman who, if spooked, would not only stomp his heart but grind it under her boot heel and spit on it. She was jumpy like an abused horse, so afraid of being hurt again that she'd fight against caring.

But she did care. For her family. For the dogs and the horses. For him, too. Her encouragement on the project kept him going. And having her along to make introductions to townspeople had proved invaluable. He knew the questions and stares made her uncomfortable, but she'd gone with him anyway.

Beneath that crusty exterior was a woman who could either break his heart or make him the happiest he'd ever been.

"Tomorrow evening I have a date," he said, mostly to get a rise out of her.

"Have fun." Holding the reins lightly, Monroe stared straight ahead into the barely lit path.

So much for stirring up her jealousy.

Nathan bumped her shoulder with his. "With a woman who played tennis with my mother."

She turned her face toward him. "That sounds promising."

"Only if you'll go with me. She claims to know you. Evelyn Brunowsky."

"Evelyn. Yes, I know her. Or used to."

"So you'll go with me to break the ice?"

"I'll check my calendar."

Nathan let the topic die. For Monroe a *maybe* was as good as he'd get. One of these days he was going to get a straight *yes* from her.

The carriage took a hard bump over a pothole, jangling the harness. Nathan held the lantern up a bit higher.

"If I didn't know better," he said, "I'd think we were living in the 1800s. But it's kinda nice."

"I like it. The world was easier then, I think. Kinder."

"Maybe. Or maybe the problems were just different and the pace was slower. That's why people will come to Persimmon Hill. To slow down and enjoy a quieter lifestyle."

Monroe slowed the horse, adjusting her hold on the reins to guide the Morgan across the pond dam. "What if you offered an optional campfire package near the creek or even an overnight campout on horseback like the olden days?"

"You're brilliant," he said, already imagining the possibilities.

Monroe snorted. "You're hallucinatory."

He bumped her shoulder with his, teasing. "But you said you like me."

"*Might* like you. Don't get overconfident."

Nathan chuckled. Did she have any idea how much fun she was? All bluster on the outside and marshmallow on the inside.

"I'm on to you, Matheson."

She glared at him in warning. "Don't get cute. I can take a man out in nine point five seconds."

"Take me anywhere you want to, darlin'," Nathan said in his best Texas drawl. "But don't rush."

Her snort became a belly laugh. Barely holding the reins, she tipped back on the bench seat and laughed long and hard. He'd never heard her laugh that way, and he loved it. He laughed with her.

If the well-trained horse hadn't known the way, they'd have gotten lost.

When the moment of frivolity ended, Nathan dropped a casual arm around her shoulders. She didn't shrug him off, so he scooted closer. "Tonight's been fun."

He felt the easy shift of her shoulders and back as she controlled the carriage. The cowgirl looked willowy and feminine but those muscles were strong.

She probably *could* take him out in less than ten seconds.

"Better than The Rooftop restaurant?" she asked.

"A different kind of better. But I'd still like to take you to The Rooftop sometime."

She didn't say anything and he didn't push. *One of these days,* he thought. Years of waiting to learn about his parents had made him a patient man.

On their approach to the house, three dogs joined them, shadowy forms in the darkness. Peabody, Gramps and Rake. The others were nowhere to be seen.

Nathan didn't know how he and Monroe had gotten away from the house earlier without the dogs trailing them. But he was glad they'd been alone for once.

Inside the lighted barn, dogs dancing around their feet, Nathan helped Monroe unhitch the carriage and put away the tack, learning the process as she named each piece of equipment and explained its use and care.

"You're a good teacher," he told her. "You'd be terrific with our guests." He'd specifically said "our" to draw her in.

She didn't take the bait. "Not happening."

"Pray about it."

"Don't need to."

He sighed. If she wouldn't pray, he would. He couldn't convince her to step out of her hiding place, but God could.

Monroe had become important enough to him that he wanted her to feel comfortable in her own skin again, the way she must have before the fire. He couldn't imagine the agony she'd been through, both physically and mentally, to go from beauty-queen status to a scarred recluse hiding her face from the world.

They finished brushing the horse and then headed him out to pasture, turned off the barn lights and walked toward the house.

"Hold my hand," he said. "I'm scared of the dark."

She made a noise in her throat that said she knew he was teasing, but she took his outstretched hand anyway. "Only because you're a wimpy greenhorn."

They stopped at the back door, but he didn't release his light grip on her hand. For a hardworking cowgirl, her skin remained smooth and feminine, very different from his calloused palm.

He liked the difference, but then, he'd have liked it just as well if her hands had been as rough as tree bark.

Man, oh, man, he had not bargained for this woman who stirred his protective side and intrigued him in ways he hadn't thought possible. He wasn't looking for romance, didn't have time for a relationship. Yet, here she was, and as much as he had on his plate, he wasn't willing to push Monroe away.

She was becoming increasingly important to him.

The three dogs trailed them to the back porch. Nathan wondered how the other two were doing. But only vaguely. His focus was on Monroe.

"This was the best evening I've had in a long time," he said.

"Me, too. Really, Nathan, tonight was…nice." She said the latter as if she didn't quite know how to react to an enjoyable, nonworking evening with him. "I thought you'd laugh at me for wearing a dress to a picnic."

Her admission told him a lot.

"Are you kidding? You took my breath away. Still do." He stepped closer. "And you smell so good."

"Like fried chicken? Or horse sweat?"

The word *deflection* popped into his head. He

didn't need a psychology degree to understand that she joked to cover feelings of vulnerability.

His chest ached with wanting to take away her fear of letting anyone close.

Facing her, Nathan reached for her other hand. "Will you punch me if I kiss you good night?"

She sniffed. "We'll see."

He took that as an invitation.

Heart rat-a-tatting like a nervous drummer boy, Nathan slid both hands through her heavy, silken hair to cradle the back of her head. Right before his mouth touched hers, he murmured, "The first dog that jumps in between us is grounded for two weeks."

Her giggle bubbled beneath his lips.

He'd made Monroe giggle. A belly laugh and a giggle all in one night. Progress.

He pulled slightly away, though he remained close enough to feel the warm waft of her breath tingling his face. "Are you laughing at me?"

She looped both arms around his neck. "Kiss me and I'll let you know if it's laughable."

He made sure it wasn't.

Monroe was pretty sure she'd lost her good sense. Last night, she'd kissed Nathan the way a person dying of thirst gulps water. Desperately.

Kissing Nathan had reminded her of all she'd lost, and yet, being held in his arms while he tenderly, insistently kissed her made her wish for the impossible.

He made her itchy in the worst way. Or maybe the best way. Monroe was so conflicted she didn't know if she was coming or going.

She'd be better off going than to fall for a rich greenhorn cowboy who didn't seem the least disturbed by her beastly scars. Was it an act? Some kind of cruel game pretty boys played with ugly girls?

Or was he the one who'd lost his senses?

This morning, after a restless night's sleep, she and her dogs arrived at Persimmon Hill. Leaving the pack to roam the freshly manicured yard, she went inside the mansion's sunroom, where she and the big boss usually met to discuss the day ahead over coffee and, when he'd gotten up early to run into town, Ms. Bea's pastries.

Nathan wasn't there.

Insecurities flew in like buzzards around a dead carcass. Picking at her wounds.

Was Nathan avoiding her? Did he regret kissing her and saying all those sweet, teasing things? Had she insulted him one time too many?

Forgoing breakfast, she brewed a single cup of fragrant coffee in his Keurig and shot him a text.

"What's up?"

"I am. Since four."

"That sounds bad. Did something happen?"

"Yes."

Before she could ask for details, her phone rang. It was Nathan.

"Hey," she said. "What's going on? Are you okay?"

"A supply truck showed up early."

"That's a good thing, isn't it?"

"Would be if he'd come to the right construction site." She could hear the frustration in Nathan's tone. "I called the supply company. Everything that should have been on that truck is back-ordered. Supply chain issues, they claim. This will throw us at least two weeks behind."

"I'm sorry. I know it's frustrating, but two weeks isn't that long."

"It is to me." There was something in his voice she didn't understand. Nathan seemed always in a rush, as if the project had a set end date and the world would implode if he wasn't finished in record time.

Monroe understood enough about construction projects to know that time was money, but Nathan took the concept to a whole new level.

"Want me to bring you some coffee? You sound as if you need it."

"Can't. I've got a dozen problems to sort out this morning. I'll call you later."

No, he wouldn't. He was avoiding her. She should have known better than to make a fool of herself last night. Wearing a dress to a picnic. Ridiculous. Kissing him, not once, but several mind-boggling times. Insane.

When would she ever learn?

By midafternoon, Nathan knew he wasn't going to make the six o'clock meeting with Evelyn Brunowsky, the woman who'd been a friend and tennis partner of his mother.

Frustrations on the job site ran high. Tradesmen were cranky. His head banging like a rock drummer, Nathan was edgy and struggled to remain calm.

For three months the remodeling project had gone well. Now, suddenly he was falling behind schedule. Delayed permits. Delayed materials. Subcontractors who showed up late or not at all.

He'd had to fire the lackadaisical plumber who clearly did not appreciate his second chance. Then he'd scrambled to find someone else, which, in turn, threw him behind on every single building.

As a man who'd acted as general contractor on projects before, Nathan knew to expect a few setbacks and delays. Persimmon Hill seemed intent on breaking the record for the most delays ever.

Was God trying to tell him something? Warning him to let go? Or was this a growing period, a trial to see if he would persevere in the face of difficulty?

God was like that sometimes. Growing him. Stretching him.

He was certainly stretched right now.

His grandparents would tell him to sell out and come home.

How did he explain that Persimmon Hill *was* home now? The longer he was here, the more convinced he became that everything he'd hungered for since he was six years old, everything he needed to learn and understand about his past and maybe his future, was right here on Persimmon Hill.

If he stayed strong and kept fighting.

In the end, if he had to sell, he'd not only be a failure, he'd be a failure with a broken heart.

As if to encourage him, a favorite Christian song floated through his thoughts. "Failure's not an option when the Father's in the room."

"Not an option," he muttered. Somehow, someway, he must complete the project on time.

Removing the baseball cap he'd slapped on his head to keep dirt out of his hair, he wiped sweat as he walked a dozen yards away from Cabin 4, soon to be dubbed Sugarberry, to a line of native oak trees. Not a leaf stirred.

Gazing upward into the hot July sky, he whispered a short prayer for guidance. Last night, he'd prayed for Monroe, prayed for wisdom in pursuing a relationship with her.

"Are these delays my answer about Monroe, Lord?" he asked. "Should I focus fully on the ranch and ease back from these growing feelings? What about my parents? You brought me here. I know You did. And I have to believe You have more for me in this place than a business venture. But the pressure to finish on time is a real issue. How do I balance all three?"

Nathan was convinced that, behind the scenes, God worked all things for his good.

Yet, he still didn't have any answers.

When his phone rang and he saw his grandmother's number, he shook his head and started back toward the cabin. The new plumber worked inside while a carpenter replaced rotting boards on the outside. The high-pitched shrill of a table saw pierced his ears.

Nathan contemplated not answering Grandmother's call. He already knew what she would say. And he was too busy to argue or risk letting his headache and short temper hurt her feelings. He didn't need the added pressure today of all days.

But he owed his grandparents so much and they weren't getting any younger. What if one of them was sick?

He answered, and then didn't know whether to be relieved or aggravated that Grandmother played the same old tune, urging him to come home.

"I can't, Grandmother. I love this property. I'm committed to return Persimmon Hill to the happy place I remember."

"You were too young to remember."

"I remember enough, and Grandmother, when I'm finished, I want you and Granddad to visit. It's a beautiful ranch."

"I will never step foot in the house that murdered my daughter." Tears clogged her words.

Though disappointment filled him, Nathan realized he'd pushed too hard, too fast. He wanted to please them and make them proud, but this was something he had to do, even if they never saw the result of his hard work. "I'm sorry. I shouldn't have brought it up. I love you, Gran."

He spent a few more minutes mollifying his grandmother before making an excuse to hang up.

"Mr. Garrison. Nathan."

Nathan looked up to find the carpenter waving him over. His text app buzzed. A burly driver hopped out of a dump truck and strode in Nathan's direction with purpose.

From the corner of his eye, he spotted Monroe on one of the newer horses. Five dogs, with the energetic Torpedo in the lead, trotted alongside.

Sweet memories of last night's picnic momentarily crowded out the worries this day had brought.

He enjoyed matching wits with Monroe. Each

time he dug beneath the surface of her toughness, he discovered a woman to admire.

Kissing Monroe, holding her fit body close, was about the most pleasurable thing that had happened to him in a long time.

He turned to wave but before he could, Monroe spun the horse and trotted in another direction. Dust stirred beneath the hooves, clouding the smaller dogs.

How could he back away from something so good?

He couldn't.

Should she call him again?

Inside the riding stable, which hadn't taken much to refurbish, Monroe held her cell phone in one hand and stared at the photo of Nathan she'd snapped for her caller ID. Even in a candid photo, he was movie-star handsome.

But it wasn't Nathan's looks that drew her with the power of an electromagnet. It was *him*, the man.

Like a teenager with a crush, she fretted that he'd guess her feelings if she phoned him too often. She couldn't let that happen. He might want to kiss her in the dark but that didn't mean he had romantic feelings for her.

Did it?

"Ooh." She made herself so mad. "Stop it. Just stop it."

The horse she'd ridden into the stable turned his long equine head to stare at her with soft eyes.

"Not you, Sid." She patted his shoulder. "Me. I'm my biggest problem. I can't like him. I don't like him. I *won't* like him."

All five dogs heard her voice and came to sit in front of her. Rake held up his amputated paw. Torpedo rolled onto his back. Peabody whined and thumped his tail. Gramps snorted. Even Goldie's missing eye seemed sympathetic.

"Should I call him?" she asked. "I'm going to call him." Before she could back out, Monroe tapped his photo and reminded the dogs and horse, "He's my boss. This is business, not personal."

None of the animals believed a word of it.

"Hey. Everything okay?" Nathan's warm baritone soothed her insecurities.

"Just dandy." A little nutty, but okay. "Did you get the issues resolved?" Whatever they were.

"Some. Where are you?"

"In the main stable. I was working with the new horse."

"Stay there." Before she could ask why, he hung up.

In minutes, Nathan roared up on an ATV. She met him in the breezeway.

"What's going on?"

He killed the machine and hopped off. "A lot and I have to get back to work."

"Right."

"But I hadn't seen you all day and didn't want you to go home until we talked."

About what? Was he going to apologize for kissing her? Tell her he'd been drunk on sweet tea and out of his head last night?

She cocked a hip. "Aw, you missed me."

"Seriously, Monroe, I did."

She rolled her eyes. "Don't get schmaltzy."

He ignored her intentional effort to regain her balance. The man definitely unsettled her equilibrium.

"I wanted to ask you to dinner tonight, but that's not possible now."

Not possible because he regretted last night? "Look, Nathan, about last night. I don't want to give you the wrong impression." She held the horse's bridle so tightly, her knuckles ached. "You're my boss. I'm the employee. Nothing personal, okay?"

A frown drew lines on that handsome forehead. "Nothing personal? Felt pretty personal to me."

"That's what I meant. It shouldn't. Given the situation and all."

"The situation?"

"Yes. You're busy. I'm busy. We're two different people."

A smile erased his frown. "Thank the Lord for that."

"Be serious."

His cell phone pinged. With an annoyed sigh, he held up one finger as if to ask her not to leave and yanked the device from his pocket.

The frown returned. He pinched the bridge of his nose. Muttering to the text she couldn't see, he said, "How am I going to juggle all this? I'm running out of time."

He shoved the cell phone back in his pocket and returned his attention to her. "You were saying?"

"What was that about? How are you running out of time?" A sudden, terrible fear gripped her. "Are you dying?"

"Dying?" His bewildered expression changed to humor. "Well, eventually, I suppose. It's inevitable, but no, not anytime soon that I know of."

"You're confusing me. What's wrong? And how are you running out of time?"

Nathan went quiet, looked to one side as if in contemplation and then back to meet her questioning gaze. "I haven't been completely up-front with you."

Monroe stiffened.

Here it comes, she thought as she struck an insolent pose, a hand on her hip and eyes narrowed. "Remember, I can take a man out in nine point five seconds. I expect the truth, the whole truth and nothing but the truth. Got it?"

A tired smile lifted just the corners of his mouth. "You called me a rich boy, remember?"

"A rich, rhinestone cowboy. Yep. That's you. Fancy hat and all." Although, in grubby old jeans and a sweaty T-shirt he didn't look too fancy right now. He looked...manly. And stressed.

Monroe did not like seeing him stressed.

"I'm neither. I have a good job back in Houston, but nowhere good enough to do everything necessary to restore Persimmon Hill."

She'd known he wasn't a real working cowboy but she'd been convinced he was rich.

He wasn't?

"Then, how in the world are you doing all this?" Monroe waved her hands around the property where half a dozen projects were ongoing.

"A loan." He removed the ball cap that she found particularly appealing and slapped it against his thigh. "A six-month loan with Persimmon Hill standing as collateral and a six-month leave of absence from my management job. If I make deadline and prove this guest ranch can turn a profit, the lenders will roll my loan into monthly payments. If I don't make the deadline, or don't see sufficient bookings, I'll have to sell Persimmon Hill to repay the money. If that happens, hopefully, my job will still be waiting back in Houston. But even that is not a given."

Whoa. She had not expected that. Nathan was in deep. Real deep.

"You can't sell this ranch." The idea of a bunch of strangers overtaking Nathan's home appalled her. "Persimmon Hill belongs with you. You have history here. This is your home and you're working hard to make it shine again."

"I agree. But the bank couldn't care less about nostalgia or my tender feelings."

"What about your family? Can they help?"

"They're pressuring me to sell everything and forget this property ever existed."

Monroe saw the sadness in his eyes and heard his worry. She understood then what she'd missed before. He was a man on a mission all by himself. Alone.

She understood feeling alone. Her heart ached for him.

A powerful desire to make things better for this good man seized up inside Monroe. All previous thoughts of putting distance between her and Nathan fled.

He needed her.

Monroe straightened, mind whirling and tone fiercely determined. "What can I do to help? Anything. You name it and I'm your girl."

Before she could say more, Nathan pulled her into his arms. His hold was light and easy, nothing too romantic, and she realized he needed comfort. She could do that. Everyone needed to be held once in a while. Even pretty boys.

Seeing this normally strong, confident man vulnerable empowered Monroe.

She stroked her hands up and down his back, over muscles honed over the past couple of months. He worked so hard, from sunup to sundown most days and often into the night in his office. Last night had been an anomaly, one they'd both needed.

In a whisper against his chest, she asked, "Tell me, Nathan, what can I do?"

His sigh was long and deep. "You're doing it."

After a couple of minutes, with the dogs sniffing at his boots, he kissed the hair above her ear and stepped back, giving a small, self-conscious laugh. "Sorry."

"Don't be. You're tired, overworked and you have so much left to do."

"Including a trip to town I need to make but can't."

"I'll go in your place."

"Just like that? No questions asked?"

Monroe's stomach tightened. Her throat went dry. What did he want her to do?

But she'd already said she would do anything to help.

"Yes," she said. "Just like that."

Chapter Ten

Long after sunset, Nathan worked in one of the future foreman homes assisting the new plumber to set fixtures and attach lines. He wasn't a plumber but he took orders quite well.

"Thanks for staying overtime, Reggie," he said to the man whose pants sagged from the tools dangling off him like Christmas ornaments.

"I want this finished as much as you do. Got another job waiting." Reggie rolled his head as if his neck was stiff. "Ready to install that tub?"

"Let's do it."

"Most general contractors stand around with punch lists and talk without getting their hands dirty. Not too many pitch in like you do."

"Owning the place makes me anxious to get finished." Among other reasons. "The more I do, the faster I can open the doors to the public."

And repay the loan. Time really was money.

As the pair of them wrestled the soaker tub

through the doors and into the bathroom, Nathan's thoughts kept returning to Monroe. He'd been both surprised and pleased when she'd agreed, without question, to meet with Evelyn Brunowsky in his place.

He hadn't heard from her since she'd left, chin set, hair covering the scars like a shield.

Was he heartless for putting her in such an uncomfortable, at least for her, situation? Or did she need to be pushed out of her comfort zone and into the world?

Fretting over the uncertainty of choice, Nathan finished the work with the plumber and waved the man home. After locking up, he rode the ATV back to the mansion. Home.

How did he reconcile feeling completely at home on Persimmon Hill with the comfortable life and successful career he'd built in Houston? How did he juggle everything?

He didn't know.

Another worry to add to his long punch list.

His head throbbed. He really needed a pain reliever.

He also needed another good, long talk with God. Worry was antithesis to faith. He knew that. Worry couldn't fix anything. Prayer could. Even when answers didn't come, prayer brought peace.

Tonight, he'd find time to be alone with the Holy Spirit, even if he had to forgo an hour's sleep.

As he drove into the now neatly mowed yard, too tired to park in the back and walk around, his stomach lifted along with his weary mood.

Monroe, surrounded by dogs, leaned her back against the front porch pillar, one boot on the porch and one on the ground, exactly the way she'd done the first day he'd seen her.

She was back. Nathan's heart thudded against his breastbone. He'd missed her. She'd been gone only a few hours and he'd missed her.

He was getting in way too deep.

"About time you showed up, lazy dog." Monroe put a hand over Peabody's scarred ear. "No offense, pal. I was talking to the greenhorn."

A fresh spurt of energy surged through Nathan. Monroe did that for him with her wit and gruff kindness.

He sat down next to her on the porch. Rake climbed onto his lap. As usual, Nathan began removing leaves and twigs from the seemingly appreciative animal.

"You might as well adopt that dog. He adores you."

"I'm thinking about it. Can you spare him?"

"Sure. I'll still see him every day."

"I like the sound of that. Every day. You here, even after we open for business."

"You planning to stick around after the grand opening?"

There it was, the question that plagued him. "I don't know if I can."

Back in the spring, his focus had been on learning about his parents and creating an operating guest ranch. He hadn't considered what he'd do once he reached his goals. Even as the mansion felt more and more like home, he still had a life and a successful career waiting back in Houston.

But every day he fell more in love with Persimmon Hill and the community around him.

What if he failed here and lost both?

The anxiety sometimes kept him up at night.

He used the awake time to fine-tune a website, pore over marketing and promotional ideas, juggle subcontractors and supply companies and figure and refigure the budget.

And pray. He was grateful that the Lord never slumbered or slept.

"I got the photos."

Her words snapped him back into focus.

"Evelyn Brunowsky? How did it go? You okay?" All alone, without him as a buffer, she'd met with a woman she hadn't seen in years. He found that particularly heroic.

"This isn't about me," she said.

Yes, it was. So very much. "Thanks for going. I know it wasn't easy. It means a lot."

She meant a lot.

Monroe Matheson was another reason he was

falling in love with Persimmon Hill. A very important reason.

The porch light reflecting the vivid blue of her shirt's Aztec design, Monroe hitched a shoulder as if to shrug off Nathan's gratitude.

"Mrs. Brunowsky is a nice woman. I recorded the things she said on my phone so you could hear them firsthand."

Smart. Thoughtful. Monroe was all the good things she tried to hide behind that curtain of hair and a smart mouth.

God, help her heal. I really care about her. Am I off-base for wanting her to feel the same?

But how could that ever work out? How did he balance a successful career in Houston with the life he was beginning to envision here?

A paraphrased Bible verse rambled through his mind. *Sufficient for today are the worries thereof.* Maybe the rendering wasn't exact but the message was the same. He could only handle one thing at a time, one day at a time.

Now if he could only remember that when he was overwhelmed.

Beneath the yellow glow of the bug light, Monroe interrupted his thoughts to hand him a folder. Then she whipped out her phone and pressed the recording.

When the woman's voice stopped, Nathan leafed through the folder of old photos, most taken on the tennis court. His mother, in a short white skirt and tennis shoes, hair in a ponytail, looked the way he remembered. Young. Happy. Beautiful.

"I'm puzzled," Monroe said. "Every single person we've spoken with, including this woman who knew your parents well and spent time with them, claims they were a devoted couple. My grandpa says the same thing. No problems. No tension. So what happened?"

"That's what I recall, too. They loved and respected each other. Their marriage was stable." He thumped the middle of his chest, dissatisfied that no matter whom they spoke with, the answer was always the same, and he was never any closer to finding out why his parents died. "I'm convinced my parents were devoted to each other, and that Dad would never have taken anyone's life, especially my mother's."

Monroe placed a hand on his forearm. Comforting him. She was good at that. Did she even realize it?

"That's a wonderful memory to cling to, Nathan."

"As strange as it may sound, I want what they had. Not the ending, of course, but the kind of loving relationship everyone says they had before…" He let the rest trail off, never quite knowing how to describe his parents' deaths. The words *murder-suicide* were too harsh.

"I suppose we all want that," she replied. "Until some jerk rips the love right out of us."

"Is that what happened to you? Some lowlife with no brains broke your heart?"

She went silent for a time and Nathan figured he'd pressed the wrong button. But then she began to speak.

"After the fire, I was hospitalized for a long while. Skin grafts, the whole enchilada—" she touched her cheek "—which clearly don't help that much. Even the grafts left scars."

She cuddled Torpedo on her lap and for once the dog remained still, sensing her distress. Peabody insinuated his big body next to her as if to shield her from hurt.

"Tony, my fiancé, came to visit once. *Once.*" The word throbbed from her throat. "Later, when I was ready to leave the hospital, he sent a text." She rubbed her fingers lightly up and down the terrier's pointed ears. "Breaking an engagement by text is a new level of cruel. He claimed my scars weren't at issue, but I knew he lied. One look at me was all it took to drive every ounce of love from him."

"If that's love, I don't want it."

"Me, either. Never again."

"Did you see him after that?"

"No. He told me to keep the ring for my trouble." She laughed, a bitter, harsh sound. Peabody whined and gazed at her with worried eyes. "My trouble. Did he actually think a diamond could make up for what he and the fire had taken from me?"

"He was the loser, Monroe, not you."

"Doesn't feel that way."

"I know what you mean. A broken relationship breaks more than contact with that person. It breaks something inside you that makes you doubt yourself."

She rolled her head toward him, green eyes understanding. "Your ex?"

"Yes. Clare wasn't a bad person, but she was bad for me. We were okay in the beginning but the cracks were already in the foundation. I wasn't who she expected me to be. She wasn't happy. I heard that a lot, and honestly, I wasn't, either, but I don't believe in divorce so I stuck it out, trying to make things work."

"I can see you doing that. The way you're doing here and for your parents, fighting for what you believe is right."

"When she left, I didn't know what to feel for a while. Angry because some guy she'd met at work fulfilled something in her that I couldn't. Devastated, relieved, guilty. Empty."

"All good reasons never to fall in love again."

Nathan removed one final tangled twig from Rake's fur and received a hand lick for his efforts.

"I don't believe that, Monroe. Maybe I did at first when the grief was still deep, but the Bible says it's not good for a person to be alone. Men and women need each other. God wants us to have His kind of love in a life partner. I want *that*. A God love, a lifetime commitment. To have kids and weather life storms together, to grow old together."

"That's what Poppy says, too. But I thought I had a forever relationship with Tony and here I am, a mess. After your ex cheated on you, how could you ever believe in love again?"

"Prayer. Getting closer to God. He's the author of real love." Knowing how trite and self-righteous his answer sounded, Nathan lifted the dog to the ground and scooted closer to Monroe. "Even though it hasn't been easy, leaning on my relationship with Jesus got me through. He was treated far worse than I, and yet He never stopped caring about people. He's my example. Don't get me wrong. I'm not perfect. I have my moments. But I still believe in lasting love and I want it."

With you.

The thought should have shocked him, but it didn't. Deep down he'd known for days, weeks. Maybe from the first time he'd seen her lounging on his front porch.

Regardless of all he had going on, he was falling in love with the tender-tough cowgirl.

He didn't say that, of course, and was immediately glad he hadn't.

Monroe's chest rose and fell in a deep, sad sigh.

"I wish I could believe that a relationship can last, but I don't."

He put his arm around her shoulders. "You can."

"I hope so. But I'm not there yet."

"Would you be offended if I said I'm disappointed? Love matters, Monroe. *You* matter. To me."

Turning his body toward her, Nathan gently, tenderly pulled her into his arms. Silently, he prayed for her inner healing and that God would open her eyes to the possibilities.

Monroe leaned her head on his shoulder, and he could feel her sadness all the way through the aching center of his heart.

Monroe wrestled the conversation with Nathan late into the night. His words indicated he was falling in love with her. Dare she trust them?

She couldn't. A man with his looks and charm would break her in a million, zillion pieces. He'd leave her for the first pretty, whole woman who caught his eye.

Except Nathan wasn't like that.

Hadn't she thought the same about Tony when he'd convinced her to follow him into the navy?

But she hadn't been scarred then.

She wished Harlow was here to talk some sense into her but it was too late for a phone call. Anyway, now that her sister had found her true love, she wasn't as cynical about men as she'd once been. Some men were selfish losers, she claimed, but some were awesome life partners.

Love had done that. A God-kind of love, the kind Nathan wanted.

The kind she wanted, too, but was afraid to believe in.

Morning finally broke through her bedroom window and, after dressing for the day, she headed downstairs, where Poppy had coffee ready and bacon sizzling in the pan.

"Morning. This is the day the Lord has made." It was one of Poppy's typical morning greetings.

Spatula in hand, he turned toward her. His white handlebar mustache pulled down in a frown. "You look like you got one flat tire and your axle's broke. Bad night?"

"Didn't sleep that well."

He held up a farm-fresh egg. "Scrambled or fried?"

"Scrambled, like my brains."

"Put your sitting britches on. Breakfast's near ready."

Monroe took the browned bread from the toaster and poured a cup of coffee before complying.

She needed to talk to someone about Nathan. Poppy was wise. Though she hadn't always done things his way, he'd never steered her wrong.

He set the two filled plates on the table and took the chair across from her.

Monroe buttered her toast while trying to figure out where to start this conversation.

"Spit it out before you choke on it." Poppy had a way of kick-starting a good talk.

"Nathan."

"Ah. Yes. Good man. Godly man. Stood right here in this kitchen and talked about his love for Jesus. I admire that in a man." He aimed his fork at her. "What's the problem? Why are you so down in the mouth?"

"I like him too much, and I can't let that happen."

"Why not?"

"You know why." She brushed her hair away from her cheek. "He thinks he likes me now while it's just the two of us working together every day, but his feelings won't last. I'll be worse off than when I started."

"Why can't his feelings last? Has he said something mean to you?" Her aging grandpa leaned forward, eyes ablaze. "If he has, say the word and I'll fix his wagon right quick."

"No, no, nothing like that. He treats me like an equal except better. Like I'm special and important. He makes me feel pretty again. He doesn't seem to even notice the scars."

"Darlin', you're a beautiful woman still. That Tony feller hurt you bad and messed up your confidence. Wish I could get a hold of that rascal and tell him what for. You're better off shut of him. You know it and I do, too."

She couldn't argue that. Tony had never made her feel the way she felt with Nathan.

"You're right, Poppy. I guess I'm scared."

"You've had some heartaches, sis, that's for sure."

"So have you. Yet, you still love the Lord and trust Him. You still believe in people. In love. I don't understand that. I can't do that."

"Sure you can. Wasn't always easy for me. I still miss your grandma and my only son. Losing them both in a year's time hit me hard. Laid me lower than a snake's belly for a while. But after your daddy's accident, I had you girls to think about."

"Which wasn't fair to you to be stuck with us."

"Why, darlin', God put you and your sisters in my life to help me, to remind me that loving people heals us." He held both hands toward her, fingers upturned. "God's love heals us. You got to let the Lord Jesus in that heart of yours deep enough to fill up those wounded spots. You got to let go of the hurt and grab hold of the good things God is trying to give you. The way Nathan has done."

"Nathan? How do you mean?" She snapped off a crisp bite of bacon and chewed.

"You think on him for a spell. Everybody's got

hurts. You. Me. Nathan. Take a good look at that young man. He's had a powerful, rough go. You lost your parents, but not in such an awful way as he did. You said he found their bodies. How horrible is that for a little child to bear?"

But bear it he did and grew up to be a stable, decent man who cared about others. His employees. His family. Her.

Was that because of his steadfast faith in God?

Finishing her breakfast in silence, she texted Nathan to let him know she was running late. Then, with the dogs in tow, she took a long prayer walk through the pasture, into the woods and down to the creek where she and Nathan had picnicked.

When she reached the firepit, now cold with ash, she perched on the weathered bench to talk to Jesus.

Peabody, the big, emotional wimp, hopped up next to her on the bench while the other dogs explored, in hopeful search of chicken scraps. He snuggled next to her, scarred head pressing against her side. She rested a hand on his massive back and began to pray.

Instead of blaming the Lord and pouring out anger as she'd done since the fire, she asked for forgiveness, for a loving heart, for her eyes to be opened to the good. The way that Nathan had.

"Even though I have scars, Father, Nathan has them, too. He's overcome so much and he's still fighting to make sense of his life in light of what happened in his parents' marriage."

But he marched forward every single day, with kindness, charm, warmth and generosity.

Especially to her.

"I've been selfish, Father, clinging to my own pain when Nathan has suffered every bit as much. Not physically, but mentally, emotionally. Yet he still loves You and people."

Pushing Peabody to the end, Monroe lay down on the bench and, knees up, toes brushing the sweet dog, gazed into the leafy trees. She felt God's presence in a way she hadn't in years. But she still battled insecurities and wished the fire hadn't happened.

She could almost hear Poppy's voice. "Wish in one hand and spit in the other, girly. See which one fills up the fastest. Pray, don't wish."

"Prayer won't erase my scars. What if I let myself love Nathan and he decides he can't stand looking at me anymore?"

Jesus has scars, too. Would you turn away from Him?

The tears came then. Not tears of pity or anger, but cleansing tears.

When her nose was clogged and her throat raw, she wiped the tears and started back to the house, knowing what she needed to do.

Chapter Eleven

~~

Ten in the morning and trouble already battered him.

Nathan hung up the phone in his office and put his head in his hands.

Monroe was never late, but she was this morning. Had he scared her off last night with his talk of Jesus and falling in love again?

Now this call from his boss in Houston, pressuring him to return to his job sooner rather than later. This was the busy time of year in construction. His clients were asking for him.

Nathan had a bad feeling that when he stepped out into his personal construction zone more trouble awaited.

He was tempted to go back upstairs, crawl under the covers, and stay there, the way he'd done that terrible morning after authorities arrived.

A wisp of memory, like a shadow quickly passing, flitted behind his eyes.

There it was. The thing he couldn't remember. He strained toward it, but it slid away. Gone.

Why couldn't he remember?

Scrubbing his hands over his face, tired and frustrated, Nathan returned to the never-ending work on his laptop.

Project management was what he did for a living. Why was his own project giving him so much grief?

After an hour of realigning subcontractors to work around the delayed materials, Nathan heard a dog bark. Pushing back from his desk, he went into the sunroom to the wall of windows and watched Monroe and her dogs amble toward him.

The dogs leaped and darted, stopping frequently to gaze back at their owner with adoration.

Some of the heaviness in his chest lightened.

The slider door opened with a swish. "Anybody working around here today?"

Nathan smiled. Yes, indeed. Monroe was here.

"Not a soul." He turned to find her standing in the doorway. His whole being leaped toward her. "Glad you could bring yourself to show up today. Slacker."

One eyebrow arched. "Getting snarky, are we, boss man?"

His grin sheepish, he rubbed a hand over the back of his neck. "Learned from the best. So what's the deal? Why are you late? Should I fire you?"

"Probably. I've been thinking. Praying, actually."

He hadn't expected that. "Keep going. I like the way this is starting."

"We can go out to dinner tonight. As in a date."

Nathan blinked. His mouth dropped open. He tried to connect the dots. Dinner? Dates? Prayer?

Was she admitting what he hoped she was? That she cared about him, too? That she was willing to step out of her fear and take a chance on love again?

Oh, he hoped so.

Not that he had time for a relationship. But the adrenaline coursing through his veins proved he'd make time even if he had to stay up all night to finish his work.

"Okay," was all he said, his heart ricocheting off his chest wall like bullets in a concrete room.

He'd learned a long time ago to let others do the talking while he figured out what was going on in their heads.

"Nothing too serious, mind you. No strings." She stuck her hands in her back pockets and sniffed in that cute way she had when she was pretending not to care. "I figure you're all right for a greenhorn and I like a good steak now and then. If you still want to."

As he sauntered toward her, Nathan held back a chuckle. She wasn't fooling him one bit. She liked him. In her own cautious way, she was letting down her guard, perhaps even trusting him.

"What? You want steak?" he asked, playing it low-key so as not to spook her. "No bottom-feeding, scavenger shrimp?"

Her mouth quivered.

Grinning, he leaned in and kissed it.

A surprised little gasp escaped her. Then she surprised him in return. Long, shapely arms slid around his neck as she pulled him closer and deepened the kiss.

Nathan had intended a quick, sweet hug and peck on the lips, but suddenly, he was kiss-deep in trouble. Every sense came alive. Outside the roar of machinery. Inside the roar of blood racing through his temples.

Monroe's lips were warm and soft and delicious against his. Her familiar scent, exotic and spicy, wove through his head and made him forget all about the problems of the day.

When at least one of them—he was certain it wasn't him—eased back a little, Nathan wondered if he'd just levitated and was returning to earth on a fluffy cloud.

She'd rocked his world. Had he rocked hers?

He hoped so. She rocked his just by being in the room.

Monroe pressed a hand to his cheek and another against his chest. Did she feel the pounding beneath his shirt pocket? Did he appear as bemused and misty-eyed as she?

"Wow," he said. "Gets better every time."

He tugged her back to him and kissed her nose.

Her soft, shaky exhale caressed his face and made him want to kiss her again. "That was—"

"Powerful?" he asked.

"Unexpected. Beautiful."

He leaned his forehead against hers and sighed. "*You're* beautiful."

For once she didn't argue, didn't bring up the scars or turn her head away.

She pressed her lips to his, this time in a sweet kiss of longing that touched every tender place inside him.

Nothing serious, she'd said. No strings, she'd said.

Who was she kidding?

That first dinner date with Nathan at The Rooftop restaurant had both delighted and shot anxiety through Monroe. She and Nathan had both dressed up. She in the red tea-length sheath she'd worn in Harlow's wedding with her hair waved and swept over one eye and her late mother's dangling diamond earrings. Nathan wore a navy suit with a blue shirt that accented his gorgeous eyes. Every time she looked at him, her breath clogged in her throat.

He'd booked a corner table in the fancy restaurant, and the candlelit ambiance played every romantic chord in her orchestra. At the same time, she worried he was embarrassed to be seen with her. Why else would he choose a darkened corner?

When she'd said something to that effect, he'd swept her onto the dance floor in front of the whole world. Or at least the world of the fanciest restaurant in southeastern Oklahoma.

That man. What was he doing to her heart?

That first official date led to others, though most were more casual than The Rooftop. The kiss in the sunroom led to kisses every time they met, which was several times a day and always extra time in the evenings.

Weeks turned to months and passed in a blur of hard work, worry about the project timeline and disappointment about the lack of closure concerning Nathan's parents. All the while, she and the handsomest, kindest man she'd ever known grew closer until she took more evening meals at Persimmon Hill in his cozy breakfast nook than she did at home. Although she used the excuse that she didn't like to cook for one and Poppy was gone most evenings, Nathan probably saw right through her. Cooking with Nathan was fun, romantic, scary.

She was headed toward a heartache. What they had now couldn't last. Nothing ever did.

Nevertheless, no matter how often she reminded herself of this fact, Monroe wound up with Nathan. She'd even dreamed about him a few times and awakened with a smile on her damaged face. Then, she'd remember all over again why he wouldn't be with her for long, no matter what he said now.

But in this moment, she was happy and making Nathan happy, too. He'd said so. She was his helper, his partner. His lady. For now.

They'd interviewed, either by phone or in person, as many people as they could find who knew Nathan's parents, but they were no closer to answers than when they'd started.

She tried to encourage him, but some days she could see that he was disheartened.

She also knew he fretted about the slow work progress on Persimmon Hill. Now that she'd learned that he was not a trust fund baby with money to burn, she fretted with him. And for him.

She'd even begun praying that God would make all of Nathan's dreams come true.

Did that mean she loved him? She hoped not. Because if she did, she'd keep that bit of news to herself. Nathan deserved better than a bitter woman with scars on the inside as well as the outside. But, oh, how she loved spending time with him.

This particular day, in a rare weather event caused by a hurricane in the Gulf, the skies opened and poured rivers of rain over the bare earth surrounding the guest cabins and homes. Sod had yet to go in. The land was a soggy, muddy mess.

This morning she drove her Jeep through the mud and downpour, leaving the dogs behind to shelter at home. As Monroe arrived at Persimmon Hill, an eerie quiet hung over the construction areas.

When she entered the mansion's sunroom, Nathan stood at the wide wall of rain-streaked windows staring out at the dark clouds, hands deep in his pockets.

"Weather's set in for the day," he said without turning around. "Maybe the week."

"Can work be done on the inside of any of the buildings?"

"Some." He turned, exhaling a deep breath, and freeing his hands. "I'm not going to make it."

"You still have two months before the loan matures, right?"

"Not enough time. Cabins 5 and 6 haven't been touched. The guest home interiors are unfinished. We can't get the flooring for another month. Half the trades have moved on to other jobs during the delay."

"It's not like you to be pessimistic." Monroe went to the beverage nook. The coffeepot was cold.

"Project management is what I do, Monroe. I know how long it takes to pull together a project this large. Delays send subs elsewhere to work. Waiting for them to return adds extra time we don't have."

Temporarily forgoing coffee, Monroe went to him then and laid her head on his chest, arms around his waist. His heart bumped against her ear. "What can I do to help?"

"Nothing." He rubbed her back. "This. I'm glad you're here."

She wanted to say she'd always be here for him.

Did he want to hear that kind of declaration?

Coward that she was, and fearing rejection, she stepped back.

"You need coffee and Ms. Bea's cinnamon bear claws. I'm going into town to get them."

As she turned to leave, he caught her wrist.

His phone, lying on a small occasional table, lit up. He glanced down at the caller ID.

"County sheriff," he said.

Her eyes widened. "Are we in trouble?"

"I have a call in to him." Nathan picked up the device and answered. After a brief conversation, he slid the phone into his back pocket.

"What's going on?" Deciding to leave Ms. Bea's pastries for another time, Monroe started coffee brewing in the expensive machine.

"For the last couple of months, I've debated contacting authorities to learn more about my parents' deaths."

She returned the ground coffee to the overhead

cabinet and glanced over one shoulder. "Why the delay?"

"Many reasons. One, I'm busy here." He perched a hand on one hip and glanced toward the window. "Mainly, I wasn't sure I wanted to read the reports. It's hard enough having a six-year-old's recollection."

Understandable. And awful. "But now?"

"I'm at a dead end. Reading those police files is my only way forward."

"What did the sheriff say?"

"Jeff Ragsdale wasn't the sheriff when the tragedy happened, but from what he told me just now, nothing in the reports will change the verdict. First responders at the time knew my parents. In their shock and frantic efforts to help, they badly compromised the scene. Evidence was lost."

Leaning her hip against the coffee nook, she asked, "So, what now?"

Nathan shook his head. "I don't know. He doesn't seem predisposed to let me see the files for myself. Nothing to learn from them, he says, so why put myself through the ordeal?"

"Perhaps he's right, Nathan."

The rich fragrance of coffee rose between them. The machine gurgled.

Neither of them paid any attention.

"My main reason for coming home to Persimmon Hill was to learn about my parents."

"And you have. You know they were good

people, well liked and respected by the community, who ran a reputable business. Can't that be enough?"

He patted his mid-chest. "I still have the feeling that something else happened that night that I can't remember. Something that might lead me to why they died."

Monroe refused to share the thoughts racing through her head. That Nathan was in denial and that his parents had died exactly as authorities had determined twenty-four years ago.

She wanted to help, not hurt him more. And he was, indeed, hurting. So many disappointments and stressors pressed in on him this morning.

He needed a change of pace.

She grabbed his hand. "Put on your hat, cowboy, and let me buy you a doughnut."

She couldn't do much but she could give him a brief respite.

"But you made coffee." He waved toward his laptop opened on the small table. "I have a punch list and phone calls."

"Ms. Bea's coffee is better and this rain is not letting up." With an intentionally sassy pump of eyebrows, Monroe pulled him toward the doorway. "Come on, you're in for a treat. I'm driving."

Nathan knew he shouldn't let Monroe drag him into town, but the fact that she'd grown more willing to be seen in public pushed him to action.

And he needed a distraction.

The beautiful, smart-mouthed cowgirl was good for him.

She was a keeper.

He rolled that over in his head, liking the way it sounded.

On the wild, muddy drive over dirt and gravel roads into Sundown Valley, Monroe played lively songs from her phone's playlist and did her best to cheer him. A skilled driver, she took curves and mud holes with speed and glee, making Nathan laugh as he clutched the dashboard.

By the time they hit the town limits, Nathan felt better, though none of his problems had disappeared.

He was not one given to melancholy but he'd let the combo of rain and delays and bad news from the sheriff get under his skin.

Once inside the cozy, sweet-smelling bakery, they chatted with the morning crowd, the proprietor, Ms. Bea, and the baker, Sage, the tall, black-haired beauty in a white apron who could turn flour and sugar into a variety of scrumptious treats. He knew because he treated his employees at least once a week.

No one they encountered mentioned Monroe's injuries. All seemed focused on the guest ranch's revival. A good thing, he thought, because he wouldn't let anyone hurt her again. Not as long as he was around to stand guard.

He almost chuckled at the image of him guarding Monroe, the tough cowgirl who, as she claimed "could take a man out in nine point five seconds." But guard her heart and her feelings he would. She meant that much to him.

They took a seat at one of the square wooden tables and debated between semi-healthy breakfast foods or stuffing themselves with apricot Danish and cinnamon rolls.

Monroe snickered when he ordered both.

A man had to eat.

Tansy Winchell, the assistant editor of the *Sundown Valley Gazette*, stood at the counter paying for a white box filled with pastries. When she noticed him and Monroe, she finished paying, then approached their table.

"Monroe, long time no see. How ya doing?"

Nathan set his coffee cup down and braced for one of Monroe's sarcastic replies or withdrawals. He was pleased when she simply said, "Good. You?"

Tansy, whose hair was striped like a skunk, grinned. "I'll be better after a few sweet rolls and a double espresso."

Monroe held up a gooey cinnamon bun. "I hear ya."

Tansy settled a curious gaze on Nathan. "Who's your friend?"

Monroe made the introductions.

Tansy's eyes widened. "So you're the one who's reopening Persimmon Hill?"

"Trying to."

"I'd love to write a story for the paper. The guest ranch reopening is huge news for Sundown Valley. Guests bring revenue to a town this small. Everyone will love you. Do you have time for an interview?"

"Why not come out to the ranch and see first-hand? Snap some photos. Monroe or I will give you a tour."

The reporter's expression turned speculative. Monroe ducked her head to one side, effectively swinging her hair over the scars.

"I'll do that. Thank you." Tansy balanced the white box on one arm. "I heard you're interested in the history of the place and collecting information on the former owners for your website. Is that right?"

He appreciated the careful way she'd worded the comment. No sensationalism, nothing about the deaths or murder-suicide.

"Yes, I am."

"I've heard a few things that might interest you, one in particular that, as a reporter, intrigued me. Did anyone mention that Paul Vandiver had been tapped to run for state legislature when he died?"

Something quickened in Nathan's gut, but he kept his expression calmly interested. Very few people knew yet that he was the son of Paul Vandiver. "I hadn't heard that."

"I wouldn't have known except my aunt mentioned it when she learned that Persimmon Hill was being restored. I checked the archives and sure enough, there was a snippet. According to Aunt Ramona, Paul Vandiver was smart and honest, and he could charm the leaves off the trees. If he wanted the job, he was a shoo-in for state senate, maybe higher office than that. Except for one thing."

Nathan straightened, on alert. "Oh?"

"His wife, Lisa, apparently didn't want him to run. Some people surmise that they argued and, well, things turned out badly."

A bite of sweet roll stuck halfway down Nathan's esophagus as he absorbed the shock of this unexpected news.

Dad had wanted to run for office. Mother had disagreed. They'd argued. Fought. Things turned sour.

Though he remembered nothing of the sort, he feared he had found the reason for his parents' deaths.

It wasn't at all what he'd hoped to learn.

Chapter Twelve

"Maybe it's not the way it sounds. Your parents' disagreement over Paul running for office and their subsequent deaths could be coincidental. Or it could have been a rumor that cropped up after the tragedy and was never even true at all."

At Nathan's request, they'd left the bakery soon after Tansy's startling announcement. His face pale, expression stricken, he said little on the bumpy, muddy drive home.

"Maybe." According to his tone, he believed the worst.

"People gossip, Nathan. They take small things and blow them out of proportion. No other person we've spoken to has mentioned anything about a disagreement over politics."

"No one's mentioned my dad running for office, either."

Monroe didn't know what to say to that, so she said nothing.

They exited her Jeep and walked up the steps to the mansion's wide, covered porch where they'd hung a porch swing and placed a cozy, peach-and-green seating arrangement.

The home once again looked quintessentially Southern country, warm and hospitable as if the lady of the house would exit with a tray of sweet tea and cookies at any minute.

Had Lisa Vandiver done that for guests?

"Want to sit and talk?" Monroe motioned to the cushioned sofa.

For the moment, the rain had eased off, though the bruised skies above threatened more downpours.

"Too much to do." Hands on hips, he leaned his head back and stared up that sky.

"They were wonderful parents, Nathan. Hold on to that."

His smile was sad. "Thanks. You're good medicine. And you're right. People gossip. It may not be true at all."

"Exactly. Everyone argues over politics. Even couples. That doesn't mean they'll do something terrible to each other."

Nathan hooked an arm around her neck and pulled her against his side. Together, they faced the stormy landscape of lushly green hills and trees, safe beneath the porch and with each other.

Safe. Nathan made her feel safe. She longed to do the same for him. He was hurting.

She placed her palm against his center back, supportive, comforting. At least, she hoped so.

"I've wondered if I'm anything like my dad," Nathan said, surprising her with the shift in conversation.

Monroe tilted her face to study his. "And?"

"Politics is an interest of mine. I didn't know Dad was interested, too. Involved."

"Enough to run for Senate apparently."

"Don't laugh, but I've considered doing the same."

Laugh? The idea terrified her. All that attention and mudslinging would make any reasonable person quail in their boots. Especially the attention.

"You have?" She choked out the question.

"Back in college, I joined a political club. I enjoyed it. It was rewarding to stand up for things that matter and try to make positive changes. Since then, I've been fairly active in various local and state campaigns. Last year, my party chair approached me about running for state legislature in the next election cycle."

Monroe gulped. "Tell me you're kidding."

Grin lopsided, his head swiveled toward her. "Don't I strike you as an honorable statesman?"

"No. Yes. I mean, why would you want to run for office? Politics is a dirty business."

"The exact reason why I want to. This country needs honest men and women to represent the people instead of themselves."

Wild horses stampeded through her chest. Politics meant newspapers and TV and interviews. Nathan's handsome face would be splashed on every news outlet and social media. Everyone he knew would be dragged into the inevitable fray. Even her.

She could not let that happen.

Although she became progressively more comfortable with locals, she couldn't bear the cruelty of those who'd compare her ugly duckling scars with the perfection of Nathan Garrison.

She'd be crushed, humiliated, and Nathan would be embarrassed by his relationship with her.

As she'd feared from the start, this man who'd won her heart would suffer because of her. Eventually, he'd be forced to turn his back on her and find someone more suitable.

Nausea swirled in her belly.

Why had she let down her guard?

She'd begun to dream again. Of a future. With Nathan.

When would she ever learn? A man like Nathan and a woman like her could never be a couple.

A tremor weakened her knees. She went hot, then cold.

Wrapping her arms tight against her belly, she fought off the painful physical reaction.

"You'd make a wonderful legislator, Nathan."

He would. The best of the best making a difference.

"Will you help me? Campaign for me? We make great partners." His arm still around her shoulders, he didn't seem to notice her negative reaction.

She hedged. "I don't live in Houston."

Letting go, Nathan turned to face her, gaze locked onto hers. Monroe dropped her head, still holding tight to her waist, lest she fly into a million pieces.

"You could," he said, softly.

What was he saying? Was he asking her to move to Houston with him? To stand at his side while cameras flashed and he made a run for public office?

He couldn't mean that. He couldn't *want* that. Not with someone like her.

"No, Nathan, I could not move to Houston. I wish I could, but I can't. You're a wonderful man, and you'd be the best possible legislator, but I…just…can't." Heart shattering, insides atremble, Monroe spun away from Nathan's sudden look of bewilderment and hurt. "Here comes the rain again. We're not going to get any work done today. I'm going home."

"Monroe? What? Hey. Wait."

With a stunned Nathan calling her name, she jogged to her Jeep and sped away.

He could run for anything and win.

But she could never run with him.

All she could do was run away.

* * *

The next morning, Monroe didn't join Nathan for their usual coffee and brainstorming. Bewildered by her abrupt departure the day before and her absence this morning, Nathan shot her a text.

Her reply was also abrupt. She was already busy in the stables.

Deciding to ask her straight out what was going on, Nathan poured coffee into a travel mug, dosed it with her vanilla creamer and headed out into a steamy, rain-soaked morning with clear, sunny skies.

Subcontractors' vehicles rumbled onto the site.

Thank goodness. Back to work. At least some of them.

His head throbbed to think of how far behind they were and how much work remained before his time expired. Last night's sleep had been restless with worry. About Monroe. The restoration. The loan and his career on the line.

He'd prayed and then negated his prayers by going right back to the worries.

What had he been thinking to try to do all this by himself?

Splattered with mud from the yet-to-be-resurfaced driveway, a white pickup truck he didn't recognize came toward the house. Ranch Properties Inc. was emblazoned in green on the side.

He waited in the side yard for the truck to

stop. Two men in business suits and cowboy hats stepped out.

Nathan grinned, tension easing a small amount. Monroe would have a field day with these two guys. All hat and no horse, she'd say.

He peered toward the stables, hoping she'd appear.

She didn't.

Puzzled, missing her, he let the two men approach him.

The tall, dark one with a paunch and a goatee made the introductions and handed Nathan a business card.

After the required niceties, the man, Mr. Frederick, said, "Nice property you have here. Quite an undertaking to restore it. How's that coming along?"

Hadn't he been thinking the same?

"We're making progress. The rain slowed us down, but today we're back on track."

A few weeks behind, weeks he couldn't spare, but that was no one's business but his.

"Our company is interested in purchasing large properties such as this. We've already researched the land and the area, so, I'll get right to the point. We'd like to buy you out. Top dollar."

The offer didn't surprise Nathan. The offered amount did.

The man named a sum that momentarily froze Nathan's breath in his lungs.

"That's a tempting offer, Mr. Frederick, but I'm not ready to sell at this point."

The man picked up on that one hint of hesitancy. "All right. I understand. But you hang on to that card and call me if you change your mind. Will you do that?"

"Sure." Nathan slipped the card into his shirt pocket. "Sounds good." His comment was mostly polite rhetoric but, in the back of his mind, he wondered if the offer was his way to avoid a financial disaster.

The men shook hands and the strangers departed. Mud splattered their truck all the way down the driveway. Nathan stared after them, his insides as jumbled as spaghetti.

Little time remained before he'd have to sell Persimmon Hill to repay his loan.

Last night he'd prayed for answers. Was this God's reply?

From the moment he'd learned of his inheritance, Nathan had believed God was calling him to Persimmon Hill for a reason. Was the only reason to learn that his father had indeed murdered his mother? Over politics?

The concept sickened him. Regardless of the newspaper woman's information, Nathan still didn't believe his dad would do such a thing.

Thinking, troubled, praying for guidance, he continued his journey to the stables.

In the distance, roofers hammered decking

onto what was to be the ranch manager's home. If the weather held, they'd replace the roof on the second house tomorrow. Situated a half mile from the mansion, the remaining home, Huckleberry House, was positioned to become a large, lodge-like guest house suitable for extended families.

The interiors of both still required paint and updates, decorations, furnishings.

He sighed, shook his head.

So much left to do. So little time.

Only six weeks remained to complete everything and open the doors to guests, to prove that Persimmon Hill Guest Ranch was an income-producing property worthy of the loan extension.

Maybe he should sell while he could and go home. Back to his life in Houston. To his career.

Jack wouldn't hold his top-tier position forever. He'd worked hard to move up in the management company. He didn't want to lose his career, but he didn't want to lose this property either.

Or Monroe.

She'd become the main draw to Persimmon Hill. Monroe and his late parents.

Entering the stable, he walked along the clean breezeway where freshly strawed stalls and gleaming silver feed buckets, courtesy of his cowgirl, awaited horses and future guests.

With a little help, she'd turned this weathered building and the other horse barns into state-of-the-art facilities while maintaining the rustic Western feel that guests would expect.

She trained and cared for the horses, kept the barns in tip-top shape, planned and cleared riding trails, ordered and organized tack, equipment, feed. Her hard work and expertise in developing a working ranch had freed him to focus on the rest of the project.

Did she even know how valuable she was?

Especially to his heart.

"Monroe," he called.

Halfway down the corridor, she appeared in the doorway of an open stall, expression flat, unwelcoming. She dipped one hip as if his interruption annoyed her.

"Good morning." He lifted the travel mug. "Brought your coffee."

"No need." The chill wafting off her could give a man frostbite.

"You mad at me about something?"

"Always."

Her smart-aleck answer cheered him a little bit. "What did I do? Tell me so we can kiss and make up."

She didn't react to his attempt at humor. "I'm busy, Nathan. *We're* busy. We should stay focused on getting Persimmon Hill finished and opened."

He couldn't argue that, but something was wrong between them and he needed to know.

"I'll always find time for you, Monroe," he said

softly, touching her shoulder because he needed the connection. "No matter how busy life gets. You and me, we're important together."

She closed her eyes as if the words were sharp pinpricks, and then edged away from his touch.

His hand fell into the empty space. Lonely. He wanted her in his arms, not an arm's length away.

Before he could dig deeper to understand why she behaved so strangely, his phone vibrated in his pocket.

He emitted a low growl. "Some days I want to throw this thing in the dirt and run over it with a bulldozer."

Though he expected a snort or an acidic reply, Monroe said nothing.

Something was definitely wrong.

The sheriff's office ID flashed across the cell phone screen.

He quickly answered.

After a brief conversation, he disconnected, his already-twisted insides turned upside down and wrong side out.

As he replaced the phone in his pocket, his fingers trembled, whether from excitement or dread, he didn't know.

Monroe shifted toward him. "Are you all right?"

They were the first friendly words she'd spoken to him today.

He studied her face, comforted to see real concern in her olive eyes.

"I'm not sure. That was Sheriff Ragsdale. He found a box of files on the Vandiver case. Claims they're puzzling, whatever that means, and thought I'd want to see them."

"Does he know who you are?"

"He's a trained cop. I think he's guessed." Nathan ran a hand over the back of his neck. "What could be puzzling in those files? Will it change the verdict we heard yesterday?"

Please, God.

"Only one way to find out," she said.

Eager to know while also dreading the details, he stepped toward her, reached for her hand, needing her now more than ever. "Let's go. The workers are here. They don't need us for a while. Come with me."

Please. I need you.

She pulled away. "You go ahead. I can't."

"Can't or won't? Monroe, talk to me. What's wrong? Why the sudden cold shoulder?"

They'd been getting along so well. Falling in love, for goodness' sake. Weren't they?

"Nothing is wrong, Nathan, other than we're too personally involved, and I'm not ready for that." She looked down at her boots. Her throat convulsed as if the words inside struggled to get out. "From now on, we should keep our relationship strictly professional."

Before he could get his chin up off the ground, she hurried inside a stall and closed the door.

Too personal? What was she talking about? They were a couple. He was in love with her. She knew that, had known since the romantic picnic. Didn't she? He wasn't a man who went around kissing employees.

With every day, he fell more in love with her and thought she felt the same.

What in the world had happened?

He was no kid. He knew the signs and symptoms of love, and he and Monroe were definitely on their way to something special.

Was she telling the truth? Or running scared?

Bewildered and hurt by her sudden change of heart, Nathan left the stable and headed into town. With or without her, he needed to examine those files.

He'd have preferred to be with her.

Apparently, she didn't feel the same.

So why did he keep thinking she did?

Monroe saddled Frosty, a white horse in need of a workout, as she fretted over Nathan.

She couldn't get his changing expressions out of her mind. First, he'd been excited about the sheriff's call. Then, he'd been hurt, confused. Because of her rejection.

She had rejected the finest man she'd ever known, the man she loved whether she wanted to or not. Letting him go now was the best thing for him, wasn't it? He deserved a beautiful, gracious, eloquent woman beside him when he ran for public office. Or even when he opened this guest ranch.

She was none of those qualities.

But she'd hurt him. And he didn't understand.

Not in the mood for a ride, she made a disgusted noise and unsaddled Frosty. Poor horse must think she was losing her mind.

The squatty senior dog, Gramps, waddled inside and plopped on the freshly scrubbed concrete breezeway. He wheezed and puffed like a steam engine. Peabody followed, back end in submissive motion, tail pitifully between his legs, as usual. Would the poor, battered dog ever recover from the damage to his confidence?

Will you?

The thought came out of nowhere. Or maybe from God. Because Monroe suddenly realized she was a lot like Peabody, constantly afraid of being hurt again.

They were both as scarred on the inside as they were on the outside.

"Poor baby." She rubbed his wide head, scarred by former owners who'd tried to make him fight and then beat him when he wouldn't. "What are we going to do with ourselves?"

And what was she going to do about Nathan?

Rubbing and patting each dog, she pondered the past fifteen minutes. He'd looked so hurt, so alone.

Thanks to her, she supposed he was both.

Alone to look into his parents' untimely deaths.

Why had the sheriff termed the files *puzzling*? Was Nathan about to see or read something that would rip out his soul and leave him broken? Hadn't he suffered enough?

"Lord, don't let him see the pictures."

She froze on the thought. Nathan was about to read a police report that could be nothing less than horrific. The crime scene photos would be even more gruesome, and they were of his much-loved parents.

"Oh, Nathan."

He'd asked her to go with him for a reason—he didn't want to face those files alone—and she'd refused.

Anyone with an ounce of mercy would have understood. But her concern had been only for herself.

"I am a selfish jerk."

Setting her chin like flint, Monroe shoved aside her own misgivings and focused on the man who held her heart.

The man who needed her at his side.

"Boys," she said to the dogs, "hold the fort. I'll be back."

Chapter Thirteen

The county sheriff's office, on the first floor of the stately, buff brick courthouse at the end of Main Street, bustled with activity as Nathan waited at the counter for Sheriff Ragsdale.

"He'll be right with you." The uniformed woman manning the desk motioned him toward a bench against one block wall as she cradled a landline telephone receiver against one ear.

Nathan, too antsy to sit, walked to a bulletin board tacked with newspaper articles about the heroism of two officers alongside wanted posters. Nathan found the contrast grimly amusing. Good guys and bad guys. The never-ending war of good against evil.

Around him phones rang. A scanner squawked. A heavy side door opened with the click and buzz of a security entrance. A woman wearing heavy perfume walked past him and left a trail that turned his already churning stomach.

Nathan tapped his foot up and down, jiggled the truck keys in his pocket, anxiety rising with every waiting moment.

His breath shortened in his lungs.

What was he about to encounter? Could he bear it?

Leaving now was still an option.

If he left, he'd never know.

"Mr. Garrison? Nathan?"

Nathan spun toward the woman at the desk. "Yes, ma'am?"

"Take the second door on the left." She motioned down a hallway of doors.

He'd already gone through the security check. All he had to do was traverse the hallway and go inside that room.

Did answers await? Or only more questions and grief?

What had the sheriff found puzzling about those files?

No matter the results, he *had* to know.

Swallowing the knot in his throat, Nathan followed the officer's directions and entered a room that looked like every crime drama he'd ever watched. A plain cardboard box marked *Vandiver* sat in the middle of a long, otherwise empty table.

The door opened behind him. Sheriff Ragsdale, a broad-chested man in his forties wearing a tan uniform, poked his bald head in. "Those are the files on your parents."

"My parents? You know who I am?"

"I'd be a pretty lousy detective if I couldn't put two and two together. You're asking a boatload of questions around town about the Vandiver case. You also look a lot like your dad's photos."

"Yeah." He'd noticed but hadn't expected anyone else to.

The sheriff motioned to the box. "Files weren't digital back then. You sure you want to do this?"

Nathan gave a short huff. "No, but I need to."

"Understandable, I reckon. I'll leave you to it, then. Let the officer up front know when you're finished and she'll put these away."

"You aren't going to stay and watch, make sure I don't abscond with evidence?"

Ragsdale motioned toward a mirror. "This is an interrogation room with cameras. Another officer will be in soon."

In other words, he was being watched.

"Thanks. I appreciate this." Nathan rubbed a hand over the back of his neck and stared at the box as if expecting a cobra to rise up and strike.

The sheriff left. The door sucked closed with a metallic hiss.

Heart thundering so that he edged toward hyperventilation, Nathan forced a deep, slow inhale and exhale. He pulled out a chair and slid onto the seat before his wobbly knees gave way.

Dragging the box toward him, he waited for several minutes with both arms around the information that would either destroy all hope or give him closure.

He'd felt alone most of his life. But he'd never felt as alone, as isolated, as he did in this moment.

Slowly, Nathan reached for the brown cardboard lid.

The door swished opened again.

He let the lid drop and turned his head toward the entry.

Every cell in his shaky body leaped toward the woman in the doorway.

She'd come.

"Monroe." He breathed the word, achingly pleased to see her standing there with compassion in her eyes. Not pity. They both despised pity. Compassion. And something more.

Tough cowgirl cared. He'd known it. He hoped her presence meant she finally knew it, too.

Monroe sniffed, one hip dipped in an insolent posture he now recognized as defensive. She was nervous, but she'd come. For him.

"Figured you'd need someone here who could read above kindergarten level."

His lips curved, spirits rising. She was exactly who and what he needed.

"I'm glad you're here. I—" He waved toward the box. "I can't seem to open it."

She rolled her eyes upward. "That weak, huh?"

She had no idea. Or maybe she did. And the

sarcasm was her way of easing the terrible heaviness of what he was about to see.

Instead of sitting across from him, she chose the chair at his side and pulled up close. Their knees collided. She grappled for his hand, squeezed and released. Her leather-and-spice scent settled in the sterile, muggy room, comforting.

How he needed this. Needed her.

Since the day his parents' died, his hunger to know and his grandparents' refusal to talk had isolated him.

With Monroe he was no longer alone.

The biblical word *helpmate* entered his head. The term perfectly fit the woman at his side.

"We got this, Garrison." Olive green eyes suddenly solemn, she added, "I'm sorry for earlier. Bad timing."

"Does this mean we're okay?"

Without answering, Monroe turned her attention to the files and scooted the box to her side of the table.

Monroe's thoughts raced as she searched for a way to shield Nathan from anything too horrible. But then, it was all going to be horrible, wasn't it?

"Let me look in the box first." She reached for the lid.

He put a hand over hers. "I don't know what we'll find in there, Monroe. Are you sure you want to look? Being here with me is enough. You don't have to go any further."

"Aren't we a fine pair, both of us worrying about the other's tender feelings?" She kept her tone sassy, but inside she ached.

Anything that hurt this special man hurt her, too. She understood that now. An hour ago, in the barn, reality had smacked her upside the hard head. Here was a man worth risking her heart.

She reached into the box and lifted out a stack of ordinary manila file folders.

"Anything else in there?" Nathan tilted the box. Something thumped against the side.

Several items, including a plastic-bagged pistol, rested in the bottom.

Gently, she righted the box and pushed a file folder into the space between her and Nathan. No need to focus on the gun. They knew it was the murder weapon.

She shivered, though the room was stuffy and the air thick.

Nathan swallowed, the anxious gulp moving her to touch his arm.

"You okay?"

"Yeah." He flipped the folder open. A police report lay on top.

Monroe frowned at the page. "Why is everything blacked out?"

"Not everything, but a lot." His bewildered tone matched hers.

She opened another file and saw the same heavy redactions. "Why redact a domestic violence investigation?"

"Good question. Now I understand what Sheriff Ragsdale meant by puzzling."

A uniformed officer stepped inside the room, but remained against the back wall, arms crossed over his chest, saying nothing.

Monroe knew most people in town but she didn't recognize him. They exchanged nods.

Returning her attention to the reports, Monroe read the unredacted sections out loud.

After a few pages, Nathan blew out a frustrated breath. "Most of this I already know."

He reached for another, yet unopened folder. Monroe spotted the edge of a photograph and put her fingers over Nathan's, stopping him. "Don't look at those, Nathan. Seeing your parents that way won't help anything, and you'll have that memory in your head forever."

He looked at her with tragedy in his eyes. "I already do."

Of course he did. He'd found them that morning. His mother. His dad.

The terrible admission sliced through her soul.

Monroe pressed her lips together, fighting off the urge to sob for the little boy he'd been.

She swallowed hard and said, "I'm sorry, Nathan. I wish I could lift this off your shoulders."

"Thank you, but I wouldn't put this on anyone

else, especially you." Nathan touched her cheek with the back of his fingers. "I'd prefer you didn't look."

Batting her eyes against repressed emotion, she nodded. "Then, I won't."

God, help him. I can't, but You can.

Nathan, fingers trembling the slightest bit, grasped the edge of the file.

Sheriff Ragsdale entered the room.

Nathan's hand relaxed. He left the photo file closed.

"Monroe." The sheriff nodded in her direction. "Didn't see you come in."

"Tracey buzzed me in. How are you, Sheriff?"

"Tolerable." Their exchange was more habitual courtesy than interest. "A real mystery, aren't they?"

He hitched his chin toward the files spread across the table.

Face pale, Nathan pushed the photo file away and leaned toward the sheriff. "You don't know why the reports are redacted?"

"I wasn't around back then. Makes no sense to me, either, so I put in a call to the former sheriff, Tom Haskell. He was real intrigued to hear that the Vandivers' little boy turned up after all these years asking questions."

"Do you think he'd talk to me on the phone?"

"I'll do you one better than that, my friend.

He's on his way here. Says he needs to see you in person and set things right, once and for all."

A frown pulled between Nathan's eyebrows. "What does that mean?"

The sheriff raised both hands. "Beats the tar outa me. I'm curious, too. Said to give him forty-five minutes or so. He's living over on the Texas line somewhere these days."

"Okay. Thanks, Sheriff."

Relieved by the reprieve, and aware that God had instantly answered her prayer, Monroe placed each file back into the box and closed the lid. "No use looking anymore until he gets here to explain."

"You'll get no argument from me." Nathan pushed his chair back and blew out a relieved breath. "Let's go for a walk or something until he arrives. I need to clear my head."

"The city park is down the block."

"Lead the way." In a scrape of chairs on concrete, Nathan and she stood.

"You two go ahead," the sheriff said. "I'll keep the files handy and this door locked until Haskell arrives." To Nathan he said, "I have your phone number. I'll give you a call."

More relieved to escape the oppressive interrogation room than she wanted to admit, Monroe reached for Nathan's hand. His strong, calloused palm gripped hers.

Touching Nathan settled something inside her.

Grounded her. As if the earth was steady on its axis and all was secure whenever the two of them connected.

So much for keeping her distance.

What was she going to do about this man and these feelings that refused to go away?

The small-town park was quiet this time of day. Nathan and Monroe walked along the winding, narrow creek draped with pecan trees and fragranced with the gentle scent of crepe myrtle.

Nathan held to Monroe's hand, grateful for the contact and her presence. They said little at first, both apparently processing the bizarre turn of events.

His head spun with more questions than he'd brought with him.

Speculation sent him in directions he didn't want to go. What had happened that police wanted to hide? Their missteps? Or something more sinister and ultimately more distressing about his mother and dad?

Until they learned what the former sheriff had to say, he'd hit a dead end. Another one. Best not to speculate.

"Hey." Monroe jiggled his arm. "You okay?"

He sighed, long and loud. "Yeah. Yeah. Sure."

"You're really bad at lying. I need to give you lessons." She stopped in the middle of the concrete trail and turned toward him. "First, you need a poker face, no emotion, not even an eye-lid flicker."

"So you're an expert?"

"Of course."

She pulled a silly face, and in spite of the tight-ness in his chest, he grinned. She was trying to cheer him. He loved her for it.

Loved her.

Whatever caused Monroe's cold behavior this morning had apparently been forgotten or set aside. Nathan preferred forgotten, erased and back to the warm relationship they'd built over the past few months.

He wasn't just falling. He'd already hit bottom and lay there in a heap, his heart outside his chest, waiting for her to claim it as her own.

He loved her.

The words kept flowing through his head like a banner.

He hooked an elbow around Monroe's neck. "Having you with me today means a great deal, and *that's* no lie."

"I couldn't let you look at those files alone."

He kissed the side of her hair. "Most of my life I've felt alone. You changed that."

Her eyes narrowed in mock threat. "Are you calling me a nuisance?"

"Seriously, Monroe." Let down your guard and hear me for once. "You're one of the best things that ever happened to me. As crazy and difficult as this is, you've made facing whatever comes my way, either here or at the ranch, easier."

Though her shoulders tightened at the compliment, she didn't pull away.

"Good. I'm glad."

He knew Monroe struggled to express tender feelings. But today, she'd told him in a dozen different ways that she cared for him.

"No matter what the sheriff tells me," he said, "and even if I don't make the deadline on the ranch project, I'll always be grateful for everything you've done. For knowing you."

"You're not giving up on the ranch." She skipped right over the personal comment and shot to Persimmon Hill.

"Not unless I have to, but things are not looking good right now." His heart would break to let go of his father's dream, his dream now, but a man had to face reality.

Monroe motioned toward a wrought iron park bench and they sat, surrounded by purple crepe myrtle blossoms and bracketed by two green trash bins.

"Don't give up, Nathan. We still have time."

He loved the way she said "we," including herself in his goals, the way he had come to include her. He could not imagine Persimmon Hill without Monroe.

"Did you see the truck pull in this morning with the two men in cowboy hats?"

"No." Her head tilted. "Why?"

Discussing the ranch distracted him from the anxiety of waiting for the sheriff. He told her about the offer to purchase Persimmon Hill.

"Don't do it. Please, Nathan, don't sell."

He stared down at his upturned palms, calloused from months of hard physical labor. A labor of love he could not easily leave behind. Two loves. The ranch and Monroe.

"What if I have to?"

"You won't. *We* won't. I'll help you. Whatever is needed to reach the finish line, we'll find a way." She jumped up from the bench. Nathan joined her. "Don't sell Persimmon Hill to strangers. It will break your heart. And mine."

She was right about that. The longer he stayed, the harder it would be to leave. As much as he appreciated his career in Houston, his heart had settled on Persimmon Hill.

"The clock is ticking," he said, sad to admit the impending failure. "We can't stop time."

"So? We work faster, get more people on the job."

"I can't afford to hire any more subs, Monroe, even if they were available. The budget is stretched to the max now."

"There has to be a way." She waved her hands, as if she could snatch a solution from the air. The long, loose sleeves of her turquoise blouse fluttered. "I don't know. Something. The town needs the guest ranch, too. I think people might help if I ask. I could organize a volunteer brigade… or something."

"You'd do that for me?" He'd wanted to say, "for us."

The import of what she offered was not lost on either of them. For Monroe to throw herself on the sympathies of the public would activate every fear that kept her in hiding.

He knew then that Monroe cared more for him than she could admit. Regardless of her bluster, Monroe not only had his back, she had his heart, and he was confident he had hers. Getting her to look past her burn scars and her fiancé's rejection to admit she cared was the challenge.

Chest filled with tenderness, Nathan stopped in the middle of a curvy sidewalk to face her.

"You are amazing."

Monroe snorted. "You are deluded."

His lips curved. He looped both arms loosely around the dip in her waist and laced his fingers behind her. "These past months with you have been some of the best of my life."

"You should get out more."

Oh, that mile-high wall of hers. How could he get her to look over the top and see inside his heart?

"I'm right where I want to be. With you. Your support, your company, even your sass today and every day, keeps me going. I don't want to lose

Persimmon Hill. But more than that—" he leaned his forehead against hers "—I don't want to lose you."

Monroe's pulse ticked inside her throat.

Oh, this man. This man.

What was he saying? What was he asking of her?

He could not possibly want an angry, damaged soul like her.

Except, she didn't feel so angry anymore. Just scared.

"You can have your pick of women." The words throbbed from her throat, unintentional, but revealing the fear she could not shake. That she was not enough, could never be enough, especially for Nathan.

He was movie-star handsome and charming. She was not.

"Even if that was true," he said, "I'd still pick you."

Monroe's throat ached with longing to believe, but insecurity swamped her.

Loving Nathan meant exposure, stares and questions. It meant taking a chance that he was not like Tony or the dozens of other people who'd treated her differently after the fire.

If Nathan ran for political office, she would be on exhibit like a circus sideshow. People were cruel. They'd ask questions, make hateful comments about how mismatched she and Nathan were as a couple.

"Oh, sweet Nathan." She touched his cheek, felt the beginnings of today's whiskery growth, inhaled the scent of his aftershave. "What am I going to do about you?"

A smile tilted the corners of his lips. He bracketed her face with both hands. His fingers found the thick scars along one side.

Monroe pulled away. No one touched her scars. No one ever had but her and the docs.

"Nathan, no. Don't."

Nathan tugged her back to him. Insistently, eyes holding hers, he explored the road map of her cheek. Just when she thought she'd die from the tenderness in his touch and expression, he pushed her hair aside and touched his lips to the scars.

Tears burned in the back of her eyes.

"You're beautiful, Monroe," he whispered against her damaged ear.

She shook her head. "No."

She'd once been beautiful. She knew how beautiful felt.

"Yes," he said, restraining her with such gentle care that she wouldn't have run away even if her weak knees had let her.

"Your scars are precious, Monroe. Precious, like the scars in Jesus's palms. They're a reminder that, like Him, the world has hurt you, but you're strong. You're an overcomer."

Emotion seized up inside her like a tidal wave. Poppy had said something similar about her scars and those of the Savior.

Was this God's way of confirming that, even if her face was no longer beautiful, she was worth loving? That love was worth the risk of exposure? That, even scarred and broken, she could be the woman Nathan needed at his side, regardless of what career path he journeyed?

Tears she'd been fighting broke loose and rolled over her cheeks. Nathan wiped them away.

"You are the kindest man I've ever met."

His smile was tender, his gaze softly teasing. "You should get out more."

She puffed a half laugh, half sob. "That's supposed to be my line."

He'd been through so much in his life and yet, he'd risen above the sorrow to show love and compassion for others. For her. *He* was the overcomer.

Honorable and decent, Nathan would be beautiful even without his movie-star looks.

Could someone like her really win the heart of a man as special as Nathan?

If anyone deserved to love and be loved, it was him.

Gathering the courage that had carried her through months of recovery, she opened her mouth to tell him.

Nathan's cell phone buzzed.

It was the sheriff's office.

Chapter Fourteen

Tom Haskell was a sick man.

The former sheriff, an angular fellow in his late seventies, maybe eighty, sat at the table inside the interrogation room, waiting for their arrival.

When Nathan and Monroe entered, he pushed to his feet, a tad wobbly but with determination in the tight clasp of his jaw.

Though his cheeks were sunken and his skin ashen, his handshake was firm and his voice steady as introductions were made.

He studied Nathan with keen observer's eyes. "I'd have known you anywhere."

Nathan couldn't say the same. "You remember me?"

"Son, a man doesn't forget something like what I saw that day."

The implication pierced through Nathan, a reminder of why he was here and where both he and the old sheriff had been. "I suppose not."

Nathan pulled out a chair for Monroe and then sat next to her across from Haskell. He wanted her close. He needed her. She steadied him, gave him confidence to face whatever came.

Did she even realize how important she was?

Leaning both forearms on the table, Nathan clasped his hands together and steepled his fingers in silent prayer. "What can you tell me? Why are the reports redacted?"

"That's a long story."

"I've waited a long time to hear it."

"Yes, you have, son. I recall seeing you that morning. I knew who you were, of course. Everybody knew your folks. Fine people."

"Yes, they were." He swallowed, nerves ticking against his collarbone.

"Nobody expected what happened," the old sheriff said, "and that was a good thing. This county is generally quiet. The unexpected doesn't happen here. Except, twenty-four years ago, it did. In thirty years of law enforcement, this was the strangest case I ever worked."

Nathan frowned. "Strange? How? I don't understand."

"You were a little child. We tried to shield you as much as we could. Though shaky and pale, you were brave as a lion. You broke all our hearts that day. Sweet little fella. Made us hug our own families a little tighter when we got home."

"I don't remember being brave."

"You had the good sense to dial 9-1-1 and then stand guard over your parents' bodies until paramedics arrived. I'd call that brave."

"All I remember is the awful realization that something terrible had happened to Mother and Dad." Nathan felt the press of grief in the back of his throat. He cleared it. "I knew they were dead. Somehow I understood that much. Then, I ran upstairs and hid under the bedcover."

"Which was where the marshals found you when they arrived to take you to your grandparents."

"Marshals?" Frown deepening, he sat up straight. "I thought Grandmother and Grandpa came to get me."

"No, sir. Two US marshals gathered you up in a quilt and drove you to Texas. I'm not surprised you don't remember. You were in shock and had fallen asleep when they got here." He shook his head. "Sad thing. Sad."

Nathan stared at the man's gaunt face. Something clicked inside his brain. The vague sense of being carried. Men talking in the front seat of a strange vehicle. Snatches of scary, horrible conversation he could barely comprehend. Not by his grandparents or anyone he knew. By two men with guns. Strangers.

Then, he'd awakened at his grandparents' home, convinced somehow that Grandmother and Grandpa had driven him there.

"Why were US marshals involved?" Monroe asked as Nathan tried to put the pieces together. "Wasn't this a domestic situation?"

"No, ma'am. It was not. Never was. What you've been told, what everyone was told, is pure fabrication. That's why I'm here. That's the choice I made that morning. I've carried the lie all this time, and it sits mighty heavy." His eyes grew glassy. "When a man's reaching the end of life, he wants to be sure he's made things right with God and man. I've done the first. For a while, I wondered if I'd get the chance to do the second. Sheriff Ragsdale's phone call was a gift from God."

Nathan's pulse picked up speed. He'd been told a lie. Did that mean his dad was innocent? "What happened?"

"The Vandivers were fine people. I intentionally muddied their good names and ruined a dead man's upstanding reputation with an outright lie." Haskell waved a bony hand in the air as if to ward off protests. "Oh, I thought we were doing the right thing at the time. Your folks were gone and we wanted to protect you. You were alive. They weren't."

Nathan's frown deepened. "Protect me from what?"

"That's where the strange part comes in. As well as the Marshals Service." Haskell leaned back in his chair and rested a minute, his breathing short and shallow. The story had cost him.

Though his mind spun in wild circles, grasping for answers, for understanding, Nathan waited patiently for the man to catch his breath. He'd been waiting for years. What were a few more minutes?

Finally, Haskell said, "Your mama had a secret that even her husband didn't know."

Another shock hit Nathan. His mother kept secrets from Dad? About what?

Afraid he knew the answer, but unwilling to accept such a thing about his beloved mother, he braced himself for a sordid tale. A cheating wife. A jealous, angry husband.

Did he really want to know?

The truth will set you free.

The bit of paraphrased scripture sprang out of nowhere, but he grabbed on to it. Sometimes truth hurt, but, he knew for a fact that lies and half-truths kept a person in bondage.

"We heard she didn't want Dad to run for political office," he said. "Was she afraid this secret she had, whatever it is, would be exposed?"

"Yes."

Nathan gulped down the bitter taste of disappointment. That was not the truth he wanted to hear.

"I loved her, Sheriff. She was wonderful to me. I'd like to preserve that memory."

"Hold on. Let me finish."

Nathan sat back. "First, tell me straight out. Did my dad murder my mother?"

"No. Paul Vandiver was a completely innocent victim."

Slumping into the chair, Nathan closed his eyes. Monroe touched his arm with her fingertips, comforting him. God love her. She could read him like a book.

"Thank God. I never believed Dad could do such a thing. He adored Mother."

"Yes. He and your mama died trying to protect each other and you. That's when my office took up the mantle of protection. Crime scene evidence was lost trying to save them anyway, and when the US Marshals Service appeared out of nowhere, insisted on secrecy and rushed you out of there, I made an executive decision to seal the reports and issue an official statement of murder-suicide. The Marshals Service didn't object."

Nathan rubbed a hand over the back of his neck. "I still don't understand. If Dad is innocent, who killed my family?"

"Some real bad people, son. Criminals." Haskell shifted his bony frame on the hard plastic seat. "You see, when your mother was nineteen, she went into the federal WITSEC program."

Shock waves vibrated down Nathan's spine.

Beside him, Monroe shifted. He felt her eyes on him.

"Witness protection?" His gentle, gracious, quiet-turned mother?

WITSEC. He'd heard that word the night his parents died, though he hadn't remembered until this moment. His mother was in WITSEC.

"Yes, sir. Brave woman your mama. When she was barely grown and in college in Illinois, she witnessed some terrible crimes and testified in the trial of several violent gang members. They knew her and vowed retribution. So the woman you know as Lisa Vandiver was given a whole new life. Never even had contact with your grand-parents or told them what had happened. Not once. Too risky. They didn't find out until after she died."

"My dad knew nothing about this?" Nathan's blood pounded against his temples as he fought to grasp the information and unravel years of tangled understanding.

"Not that we know of. Years had passed since the trial, and your mama felt safe here in the re-mote country. Good place to hide, to marry, to have a child and a nice quiet life. She deserved that."

"Until Dad decided to run for political office."

"Right. We believe he would never have agreed to run if he'd known the danger. The killers must have seen your mama in a TV interview or some such. She became a target for assassination. Your daddy, God rest his soul, was collateral damage."

His six-year-old memory tumbled back. The events that had nagged him since that night. Not only the marshals instead of his grandparents carrying him out of the house, but they'd talked about WITSEC. They'd been upset. Mother's identity had been discovered.

All these years, the truth had been hiding inside him and the trauma and confusion had blocked it.

Nathan's stomach rolled. *Assassination. Collateral damage.* Such ugly terms. More reasons he hadn't remembered. He realized now that he'd heard the noise downstairs, too. Muffled shouts. Pops. At the time, he'd thought it was one of Dad's western movies.

Instead, his parents had been dying.

"I don't know what to say. I'm stunned. Sickened. But relieved, too."

"I figured. When I heard you were in town asking questions, I realized the trauma you must still carry after what you saw and then being told your father shot your mother and himself. You deserved to hear the truth. I needed to clear my conscience."

"What about now? Is Nathan still in danger?" This from Monroe, whose comforting hand rested against the small of his back. "Won't the killers come after him?"

"He's no longer in danger, probably never was. The gang members involved are all dead now.

Even if they weren't dead, they got the one they wanted that tragic night."

"My mother."

"Sadly, yes. In the panic of the next morning, when we learned who she was, we feared Nathan could be a target, too. I couldn't let that happen. I'm sorry, Nathan. Real sorry for doing that to your fine folks. To you."

Nathan nodded. What good were recriminations? An honorable cop had wanted to protect an innocent child. "You did what you thought best."

"We did. *I* did. Still don't know if I was right or wrong."

"In your shoes, I believe I'd have done the same."

Haskell nodded; his lower lip quivered. "Thank you for that, son. You've helped a dying old man find some peace."

"You helped a child in danger. Your quick thinking and kindness may have saved my life. Let's leave it there."

"All right." The old man heaved a heavy sigh, the weight of his secret finally lifted. He started to rise but wobbled dangerously. His ashen skin paled to white.

In a clatter of chair on concrete, Nathan leaped to his feet and grabbed Haskell's arm to steady him. Monroe rushed around the table and wedged her body beneath the old man's armpit.

Grappling for his pulse, she asked, "Do you need an ambulance?"

Haskell shook his head and braced both palms on the tabletop. "Be all right in a sec."

Nathan joined Monroe in bracing either side of the old lawman.

After a few shaky seconds, Haskell nodded. "Wouldn't object if you walk me to my car."

"You can't drive like this," Monroe said.

"Daughter's waiting. She drove me up. Bless her. She knew I wanted to clear my conscience before saying howdy to the Lord."

"You did a good thing, Sheriff," Nathan reiterated to reassure him. "I know it and I believe the Lord does, too."

Together he and Monroe assisted the trembling man outside and into a silver SUV parked in a handicapped zone.

After thanking him again, Nathan stood with Monroe and watched as an honorable old sheriff lifted his hand in farewell.

Reeling from the information overload and the joy of knowing with certainty that his parents were the people he'd always believed, Nathan turned to Monroe.

"I can barely take it in. Mother in WITSEC." He looked down at the cracked sidewalk where grass valiantly fought for survival. "Surreal."

"Stunning news for sure. No wonder your

grandparents wouldn't talk about your mom and dad."

"Once the marshals informed them, they were afraid."

"Yes. For you. Being a kid, if you'd known, you might have slipped up and told someone."

"All this time I resented them, thought they hated my dad and Persimmon Hill, when in reality, they wanted to keep me away from here because they loved me." He rubbed the flat of his hand over the ache beneath his chest bone. "I owe them an apology."

"A phone call or visit wouldn't hurt. Along with the reassurance that those gang members are long dead and you are not in danger."

All those years of fear and grief. God bless his precious grandma and grandpa.

"No time for a trip to Houston, but I'll call, and maybe now, they'll come here."

Thinking, brain swirling, he gazed across the busy street where a man and a young boy entered a barbershop. Had his dad taken him there for haircuts?

Everything in his hometown seemed familiar as if he might meet one of his parents on the street. He saw them everywhere. At least, in his heart and memory.

Now that he'd learned the whole truth about Persimmon Hill and his parents, leaving seemed unthinkable. He'd needed to come here. Now he wanted to stay.

Remaining in Oklahoma meant leaving a successful career, completing the remodel and turning the guest ranch into a livelihood.

If he left his job and failed at running a guest ranch, what then?

He'd have to start all over.

Wasn't that what he was doing here anyway? Starting anew? Giving himself and his late parents and the home they all loved a fresh start?

Jesus, show me what to do. Is this Your plan and purpose for my life? Persimmon Hill? Not Everly Project Management?

A resounding yes pushed against his rib cage. Was that God's answer?

The peace settling over him said it was.

"More than ever," he told Monroe, "I have to reopen Persimmon Hill."

"To honor your parents."

He knew she'd understand. Another reason he loved her.

"Yes, and unless doing so compromises the WITSEC program, I want to share their story and restore not only the ranch, but my parents' reputations. The truth will set us all free."

Knowing this decision was right, the restraints of the past fell away like chains. "I can't leave. We have to succeed."

"Then, we better get crackin', cowboy." She bumped his shoulder with hers. "Time is short. And we have work to do."

Though knee-deep in work at the ranch, Monroe couldn't stop thinking about the former sheriff's shocking story and the subsequent information they'd learned.

Lisa Vandiver, which wasn't even the woman's real name, had only been nineteen when she'd witnessed a heinous crime. A teenager. Yet, she'd displayed amazing courage in the face of death threats to testify against the perpetrators of that crime.

In doing so, she'd given up everything she loved and the person she'd been up to that moment.

"A woman of valor, who can find?" Poppy had quoted when she'd told him the Vandivers' story.

Woman of valor, indeed.

Monroe had never admired another woman as much as she now admired Nathan's late mother.

Lisa Vandiver humbled her to the bone. And shamed her. Life had handed the very young woman bitter lemons, but she'd done the right thing and then gone on to make a good life, married, bore a wonderful son. All with doom hanging over her head every moment of every day.

Lisa's heroism forced Monroe to face the truth about herself. "I'm a coward."

The fire hadn't only damaged her skin. It had

burned away her courage and stolen her ability to put others before herself the way the Bible taught.

"No more," she muttered to Rake, who stood patiently as she brushed his tangled fur. He licked her hand.

"Talking to yourself or the dog, sis?" Harlow exited their family farmhouse and plopped down on the back porch. She and Davis were home for a visit.

"I didn't hear you come out."

"You were deep in grumbling. What gives?"

"Persimmon Hill. Three weeks is all we have left."

Three weeks to complete the interior work, furnish the cabins and open the doors. Twenty-one days to prove to the loan company that funding Persimmon Hill was in their best interest.

Reservations already booked from the new website depended on completion.

"If we don't make the deadline, we'll have to cancel reservations. Worse, Nathan's loan will be called in and he will be forced to sell the ranch to repay the money. Even though we're exhausted, we have to find a way to finish."

"Ah." Harlow pulled a lock of copper hair over one shoulder. "So it's *we* now, is it? You and Nathan."

"I'm his right-hand woman. His foreman, so to speak."

"And I'm your sister. You can't fool me. You have it bad for Nathan, and I think he feels the same. If you aren't at Persimmon Hill with him, he's on the phone calling or texting or driving over to ask your advice." She lifted her shoulders. "We all like him. He's great, so go for it."

Monroe huffed. "No time. We're working feverishly to reach the finish line. At this point, it seems undoable. But we have to. I can't let him fail."

"I repeat. You have it bad." Harlow patted Monroe's shoulder. "Anything I can do to help?"

"As a matter of fact—" Monroe tossed the brush aside and released the dog to join the others. A quiver of anxiety mingled with excitement shot into her bloodstream. If Lisa could face her fear, Monroe could face something far less terrible. "I have an idea. Tell me if I've lost my mind."

Chapter Fifteen

Nathan stared in shock at the woman standing next to Pastor Cloud inside North Cross Church.

Not only was she at church, but Monroe stood in front of the entire congregation. Even though they'd talked on the phone this morning, she'd not said a word to him about getting up on the stage.

In a flowy, green summer dress that turned her eyes to emeralds, she was so beautiful his throat ached. As usual, her thick blond hair parted on one side and waved low over the injured portion of her face so that she looked out across the audience with one eye. Mysterious, beguiling, absolutely gorgeous.

Following an introduction by Pastor Cloud, Monroe stepped to the podium and began to speak.

"Thank you, Pastor, for allowing me a few minutes." To the audience she said, "Most of you know me. I grew up in this church but haven't attended too often since my accident. To be honest, I was angry and couldn't understand why God had let this happen to me. But a wise man reminded me that everyone has scars. Some just aren't visible."

She paused to smile toward Nathan. He thought his heart might jump out of his chest. He was that proud of her.

Standing before a crowd of people was the last place he'd ever expected to see her. What was she doing? Why?

"Now," she went on, "I realize that through the broken places in our lives, we can choose to retreat, or we can choose to grow stronger and advance. Choices. My friend has faced more tragedy than most of us ever will, but instead of giving in to anger and bitterness, he grew stronger, better, kinder. Right now, that dear friend, Nathan Garrison, is working hard to reopen Persimmon Hill Guest Ranch."

At the mention of his name, heads turned toward Nathan. All he could do was smile in return. He had no clue where Monroe was going with this.

"You've read about Persimmon Hill in the paper," she said. "Many of you have driven past or stopped in to see the progress. Everyone seems excited. I'm excited, too. This valley needs the influx of business the guests will bring. We all *need* this ranch to open and succeed."

Nathan saw her swallow. She was nervous.

He fought the impulse to rush the podium and shield her.

Help her, Jesus.

Fingering a simple cross necklace as if for strength, she moistened crimson lips and, with a quick glance his way, continued.

"Which brings me to my request. The ranch must open for business in seventeen days. We already have reservations on the books."

Nathan braced himself. He didn't want the whole town to know his personal business or about the loan he might not be able to pay.

As if to reassure him, Monroe returned her gaze to his and this time, held on.

"The problem is, we aren't quite ready to open, and there's no time or money left to hire more workers. We need volunteers to clean, carry in furniture, hang pictures, etc. Most jobs are things anyone can do. So, I'm here today to ask for volunteers."

A wave of whispers passed through the congregation.

Monroe held up a hand for silence, flashing the four ever-present turquoise rings.

"To sweeten the deal," she said, "my sister's husband, Nash Corbin of the Florida Stars football team, will be at Persimmon Hill all next week, signing free memorabilia and grilling burgers. There will be other perks for anyone who volunteers." She held up the local newspaper. "Details are in today's Sunday edition of the *Gazette* and also on the table in the foyer, along with a volunteer sign-up sheet. Working together, we can make a dream a reality and generate income for, not only our town, but this entire area. Most importantly, we'll turn a long-ago tragedy into today's triumph."

When she finished speaking, the congregation applauded and excited rumbles of conversation flowed through the sanctuary.

Nathan sat in humbled silence as Pastor Cloud stepped to the podium and encouraged everyone who could to volunteer and those who couldn't to pray for the project.

"As believers," he said, "we should encourage and support Christian businesses. When you read about Persimmon Hill's first, tragic owner in today's paper, I think you'll agree. You'll also learn about a woman with the courage to do what is right, even though it cost her everything. We need more people like the Vandivers in our community, and I'm delighted to welcome their son, Nathan Garrison, to our church."

Then the pianist began to play. The choir sang. Monroe made her way to the seat next to his. As she sat down, her body trembled visibly. Those five minutes, with all eyes on her face, had cost her.

But she'd faced her fear. For him.

He wanted to hug her. But they were in church. So he leaned close to her spice-scented ear and whispered the words he'd wanted to say for weeks.

"I love you."

Her response was classic Monroe. She shot him a death glare, clamped her red lips tight, crossed her arms and refused to look at him for the rest of the service.

He was pretty sure that meant she loved him, too.

Monroe didn't hear a word of Pastor Cloud's sermon. She couldn't even recall the Bible reference, though the verses had remained on the overhead screen throughout the service.

All she could think about was Nathan's lips against her damaged ear, whispering the words she longed to hear and was afraid to accept.

Did he mean them? Or had he tossed out the phrase in casual gratitude? People did it all the time. They loved this or that, but the words didn't really mean anything.

That was probably it. He was grateful for her help. He didn't mean *love*.

Don't overthink his motives.

But here he sat, next to her, smelling of woodsy aftershave and a pressed cotton shirt, his arm resting casually on the pew at her back.

Squeezed in like canned sardines, her family filled the rest of the pew. Did they notice how rattled she was?

Harlow probably did but blamed it on Monroe's minutes standing in front of a large group of people. Seated on her opposite side, Harlow had squeezed Monroe's knee and mouthed, "Well done."

Poppy had winked. Nash nodded.

She was rattled, all right, both by the moments speaking to the congregation and by Nathan's inappropriately timed words.

When church finally ended, Monroe wanted nothing more than to rush Nathan out the door to somewhere private and ask him if he'd lost his senses.

She didn't. She was on a mission today, no matter how distracting Nathan Garrison might be. She was doing this for him.

Reminding herself of Lisa Vandiver's courage, she manned the volunteer table, answered questions and related the true story of Nathan and his parents. All were shocked, but fascinated, to learn Lisa had been in witness protection. Such things didn't happen in Sundown Valley. Or so they'd thought.

"All the details are in today's edition of the paper," Laurel Maxwell, the local newspaper editor, said over and over again as she and her lean, handsome fiancé, Yates Trudeau, lingered in the crowd to chat.

Poppy, Harlow, Nash and Davis, accompanied

by Ms. Bea, stood sentry behind Monroe as if she needed protection.

Bless them. They knew how hard this was for her.

Though she tried to ignore Nathan, his whisper circled around inside her brain, and he never left her side. His warm personality and natural charm captivated everyone just as it had her.

Only one person mentioned her accident and Nathan changed the subject so fast and smoothly, the woman didn't seem to notice.

Why did he have to be so wonderful?

When the crowd finally dissipated, her family headed to the Country Kitchen for dinner and Monroe made her escape. She was halfway to her Jeep when Nathan caught up to her.

"Hey, hold up."

She whirled around and punched him in the arm.

He rubbed the spot, though he'd gained so much muscle working on the ranch that he probably didn't even feel her jab. "What was that for?"

"You shouldn't go throwing *I love yous* around like confetti. It's not nice. Especially in church!" She batted her eyes against a sudden influx of disgusting tears. "Just because I did a nice thing for your dude ranch is no reason to go spouting off lies. Say thanks but not *that*."

"I didn't lie." He caught her by the shoulders and made her look at him. "Monroe, I love you."

"Oh, sure, you love my help with the ranch, but you also love French fries. And I am *not* a French fry."

"No, you're not." He laughed but quickly sobered. "That's not the kind of love I have for you, Monroe. Although hot waffle fries are pretty killer."

"Stop joking." She slashed a hand at her eyes. "You're ruining my makeup. And making me mad."

"Why? Why does the fact that I'm in love with you make you angry?"

"Because." She felt pouty and petulant, two things she did not like in a woman.

"Because you love me, too?"

Monroe tilted her head back and stared up at one lonely cloud. She sucked in the parking lot exhaust and sighed.

"Yes. And I can't. You deserve better and you'll fall out of love with me the moment you know the real me or someone mentions your pathetic, scarred-up girlfriend."

Nathan stood patiently, quietly listening while Monroe blurted all the reasons the two of them could never be a couple.

Then with infinite sweetness that turned her knees to Jell-O, he said, "Nothing you say will change how I feel. I love you. The real you. Rescuer of dogs, of an abandoned ranch and a heartbroken man trying to find his way. That's the real you."

Monroe's whole body ached with the need to believe. "Really? Do you really think that about me?"

She bit down on her back teeth to stop the gush of neediness. When had she become so pathetic?

"I do," Nathan said. "When I saw you standing in front of all those people this morning, my chest nearly burst with pride. That's my girl, I wanted to yell. Look at her courage, her strength, her giant, caring heart. Isn't she amazing?"

Oh, Nathan, you melt me. I don't have an ounce of resistance with you.

"Not *my* courage, Nathan. Your mother's. And yours."

"She was a brave woman, but so are you. I love you both." He pulled her up to him. This time she went willingly. "Now, be nice and say you love me, too, and let's go get some lunch."

She rolled her eyes. "You'd better not order French fries."

Nathan caught her chin and stared into her face. "Stop it. Be serious. Please. Your actions say you love me, but I need to hear the words, too. Everyone needs the words, Monroe."

Monroe softened. She loved this man and he loved her. She saw the vulnerability and hope in his expression.

She didn't have to pretend with him. She no longer had to fight against caring too much. She didn't need to fear rejection. Not with Nathan.

He wouldn't leave when the going got tough. He'd proved that already. Steady and faithful, Nathan quietly did what was right and stayed the course, facing whatever came his way.

A man most worthy. A man who loved her.

And finally, *finally*, she believed him.

The time had come to let down her guard and invite him into her heart. And her life. Where, secretly, he already resided.

He just needed the words. And she needed to step over her fear and say them.

Touching his wonderful face, serious now, her inner alarm system deactivated, Monroe leaned close and whispered against his mouth, "I love you, Nathan."

His kiss was a sigh of relief, of love and of pure joy.

Monroe lingered in the circle of his arms in the church parking lot, stunningly aware that God, in his sweet mercy, had brought them both to this moment.

Two broken hearts now melded together into something stronger, better, with the promise of a future together.

Regardless of her anger against Him, God had never failed her. Nor had He ever left her side. He'd been with her, and with Nathan, every step of the way.

Epilogue

After Monroe's announcement at church and the newspaper article chronicling the true story of Paul and Lisa Vandiver, volunteers had swarmed the ranch every day for the remaining weeks before Persimmon Hill either opened or folded.

The town seemed as determined as Nathan and Monroe to be sure it opened.

Some of the people came to see Nash Corbin, a famous football star, and to enjoy his grilled hamburgers and hot dogs, and then stayed to work. Others were curious about the boy who'd witnessed a double murder. All were eager to see the ranch open, and enthusiastically took up the challenge to beat the ticking clock.

Nathan started early and stayed late, barely sleeping. No matter how early he started or how late he stayed, Monroe was there, too.

He already loved her. Now, he adored her. She

was the woman he hadn't known he needed. But God knew.

Every morning before the bakery opened, Ms. Bea and Sage brought baked goods for the horde of volunteers. Somehow, with all the other tasks she accomplished, Monroe made sure the industrial-sized coffeepot never ran dry and ice chests filled with bottled water sat outside each cabin.

The Trudeau men, Wade and Bowie, along with their ranch hand, Riley, and three pickup loads of laughing, joking friends toted and arranged furniture. Yates Trudeau, who'd been injured in the army, hung pictures, mirrors and light fixtures and exchanged secret smiles with his fiancée, Laurel Maxwell.

Wade's redheaded wife, Kyra, along with skunk-haired Tansy Winchell from the newspaper office, assisted Monroe and Harlow in directing the placement of furniture and stocking linens and other necessities.

Even though they all worked hard, the atmosphere resembled a town party. A labor of love.

Monroe's eager, ever-present wolf pack received dozens of belly rubs and too many hot dogs.

On the final day, with his best friend and the love of his life directing the last-minute charge like a three-star general, Nathan sequestered himself in his dad's office long enough to confirm reservations and assure the loan company that the ranch would open to paying customers and that his first payment would be made on time.

Gazing around the office while he waited for a phone connection, Nathan felt, as he always did, his father's presence.

"I think you'd like what we've done, Dad."

A cloud passed outside the window and cast a fleeting shadow over the silent, leather-scented room.

Maybe the shadow was coincidence, but Nathan preferred to believe otherwise. It felt like affirmation, a blessing.

Landline ringing against his ear, Nathan gazed upward. "Thank You for that, Lord. I want You and them both to be proud."

He finished his calls, the last one to his grand-parents, and headed back outside to work.

At eleven o'clock that night, the September warmth gave way to a cooler evening, and an exhausted, sweaty and grimy but grinning Nathan waved the remaining weary volunteers toward their homes.

"No one has an ounce of energy left." Monroe flopped onto the mansion's front porch next to the wolf pack, already sprawled in various sleep positions over the wooden floor. Peabody opened one eye. Goldie thumped her tail. The others snoozed on, oblivious to Gramps's snoring.

"We made it." He lowered his weary frame to the porch and tumbled backward, feet on the ground, arms over his head. No way either of them would sit on the nice porch furniture without a shower and clothing change. "I'm so tired, I don't think I can make the trip inside."

"Sleep out here."

He rolled his head toward her. Propped against a freshly painted white column, and though her face and clothing were dirty and her hair mussed, Monroe still managed to look pretty. And impudent.

"Wouldn't that be a sight for tomorrow's guests?" he muttered. "They drive up and find the owner passed out on the front porch in filthy clothes surrounded by a pack of mongrels."

"Yeah." She sighed, apparently too tired to come up with a snappy response. "I'm working up the energy to drive home."

"Wish you could stay. Plenty of rooms to choose from in this place."

She leaned over his supine body and kissed him. "Too much temptation."

"Not from this quarter. I'm too tired."

She laughed. He loved that sound. "First guest arrives at four p.m. See you at five in the morning for a last-minute walkthrough."

His answer was a groan.

"Dogs," she said, "come on. Load up."

One by one the dogs rose, shook themselves, stretched and followed her to the Jeep.

Nathan levered onto his elbows as she put the

Jeep in gear and headed down the dark driveway toward Matheson Ranch.

He would have smiled if he hadn't been too exhausted.

They'd done it. Together.

He sure did love that woman.

And he already missed her.

On the last Friday in September, as the leaves threatened to change colors, and a flock of geese honked overhead, Persimmon Hill Guest Ranch officially opened for business for the first time in nearly a quarter century.

After a busy morning of inspections and making certain every single preparation was in order for their first guests to arrive, Monroe exercised the handful of horses she'd use for tonight's sunset trail ride.

She could barely believe it, but they'd revived this beautiful place. She almost burst with pride in her little town and the man whose dreams were bigger than any she'd ever imagined.

Nathan's dream had become a reality.

In late afternoon, she went inside the house and up the stairs to shower and change for their soon-arriving guests. Afterward, she found Nathan in the kitchen, dressed as she'd seen him that very first day. Her rhinestone cowboy in boots, hat and black suit jacket, all decked out to impress their first guests.

She was impressed. His physical beauty never ceased to take her breath away, but it was his inner beauty that she loved.

His heart had been as broken as hers, though for different reasons. Yet, he focused on the needs and worth of others. Like Jesus had. The way Monroe strove to do from now on.

Her external scars might never fade, but, with God's help, she'd make certain her inner person was as beautiful as possible. Focusing on others took the focus off self and selfishness. She understood that now in a way she hadn't before.

Nathan turned to greet her. Monroe slid both arms around his fit waist. "Mmm, you smell good."

"That's the pizza you smell. Want some while we have time?"

She chuckled. "Love some."

They settled at the breakfast nook over supreme pizza and freshly made iced tea.

"Are you nervous?" she asked.

"Not anymore. Thanks to you, and the Lord. You helped me find answers to questions that had plagued me every day of my life. You rallied the troops on behalf of Persimmon Hill. My whole life I've searched for closure, and, at last, I've found it, back here where I began, on Persimmon Hill."

"I can't take credit for any of that, Nathan. You would have found a way. But you." Rolling a string of melted cheese onto her index finger, she smiled across the triangle of pizza. "You changed my life, opened my eyes, gave me a new purpose and showed me how foolish I was to be angry with God."

"He's always had your best interest in mind, Monroe. Even when He lets us go through rough patches, He's showing us exactly how strong we are even when we didn't know it."

"Poppy tried to explain that to me, but I didn't get it until now."

"Do you know the only thing that would make today better?"

"Tell me."

Lightly, he lifted her left hand, felt the turquoise rings on each finger and settled on one. The ring finger. Slowly, he worked the turquoise circle over her knuckle, leaving her finger bare.

"I wanted to do this before our guests arrive. *Our* guests, Monroe. Mine and yours."

Pulse picking up the pace, she put the pizza down. "Do what exactly?"

"Come outside with me to Mother's garden."

"What—"

"No questions." Smiling, he pulled her to her feet and led the way outside.

Late summer flowers she'd helped Nathan plant bloomed in a profusion of color and gentle fragrance. Hummingbirds buzzed around the purple butterfly mint. Butterflies danced lightly over giant pink hibiscus and the orange and yellow coneflowers. A pretty arch over the exterior entrance to the garden proclaimed, "Lisa's Garden."

To honor his mother, he'd surrounded a small, curving white bench with mounds of her favorite flower. A black-and-blue swallowtail kissed the blossoms and contrasted beautifully with the fragrant white jasmine.

It was here he stopped and motioned for her to sit.

"This is gorgeous," she said. "I think your mother would love it."

"She would. She would love you, too, which is why I wanted to do this here and now."

He slipped to one knee in front of the bench.

Monroe's hand flew to her lips. Was he doing what she thought he was about to do?

"Monroe Matheson, I love you. I respect you. I admire you. And I need you. Even though I'm only a drugstore cowboy who barely knows one end of a horse from another, will you do me the incredible honor of partnering with me on this ranch for the rest of our lives? As my wife?"

She opened and closed her mouth, wordless for a moment. She loved him, knew he loved her, but she'd not expected this to happen. At least not yet.

This too-handsome man with a heart of gold loved her enough to marry her, scars, smart mouth and all.

She placed the palm of her hand against his smooth-shaven cheek. "Nathan. I love you so much I can barely breathe."

"Is that a yes?"

"Maybe." Then, she laughed and tumbled from the little bench into his waiting arms, delighted at the rumble of laughter filling his chest.

Here was a man who understood her better than she understood herself.

"Say you love me," she demanded, holding his face in her palms.

"I love you."

"I love you back."

Nathan's eyes twinkled. "Is that yes?"

"A great big yes." She leaned away and poked his chest with a finger. "And you'd better not renege."

"Not even a chance, my love."

She kissed him, and he returned the kiss for long moments.

For the rest of her life, the scent of jasmine would remind Monroe of this moment when everything that went before was gone away, and she and Nathan promised their futures together.

She had never expected to feel this way again, but Nathan made loving him so easy, so right.

With her blood racing and every cell in her body shouting for joy, she pulled him up to sit next to her on the white bench.

"What about your job in Houston?"

"Would you move with me if I asked you to again?"

"Yes. And I might even let you run for office someday."

"Seriously? You'd do that for me?"

"Not *for* you. *With* you. Together." With Nathan at her side, she was starting to believe she could do anything. Even move to a big city and campaign for him.

"Wow. You really do love me."

"Don't be sassy. That's my job."

His smile widened. "Just clarifying."

Then he sobered, expression tender as a baby's skin. "Politics might be in our future, but it will be a joint decision, not mine alone. You're going to be half of everything I am or will be."

She couldn't think of a single smart aleck thing to say about that. So she let him keep talking.

"Right now, I'm concentrating on this ranch and you. I already turned in my resignation at the management firm. I am officially unemployed."

Monroe patted the side of his face, heart full.

She'd never expected to fall in love much less find a man as wonderful as Nathan Garrison. A man who not only loved her as she was, but made her feel as if he was the one getting the best deal in the relationship. She knew better, but because he expected a little sass, she said, "Excellent decision."

Sure enough, he laughed. "It is indeed. You're the best decision of my life."

Oh. There he went again. Touching her heart with his sweetness.

Then, because she was mush inside, she turned to him, diamond sparkling against his chest, and spoke from the depth of her emotions. "Nathan, my drugstore cowboy with the patience of Job, thank you for seeing past the anger and scars. You're a dream I never thought I could dream. Now, I know, with God's direction, dreams come true."

"Mine sure have." Expression soft and tender, Nathan gazed into her face. She knew he saw the scars she no longer hid from him, and he loved her anyway. Maybe he loved all the more because of them. His love humbled her, blessed her.

"You," he said. "Mother and Dad. Persimmon Hill. I thought I came here only to find answers and to restore this ranch, but God brought me here to restore me."

"And me."

"Do you think he'll bring others here for the same reason?"

"There's no doubt in my mind."

Nathan listened to the birdsong in the trees surrounding the garden and Persimmon Hill as he considered the woman who would be his wife and the task they had completed together.

In the distance, he heard a dog bark and the rumble of a car engine on the newly resurfaced road.

Yes, people would come to Persimmon Hill for rest and relaxation and to have their souls restored. Like him, and his mother before him, they'd find restoration here in this remote and beautiful place.

"Someone is coming up the driveway," Monroe said.

Filled with satisfaction, peace and exuberant joy, he stretched his hand to her and, together, they went out to meet their first guests and to begin their forever.

As they exited the white picket gate, the shadow of a cloud passed overhead.

He could not help thinking of his dad and mother and of how pleased they'd be that he knew the truth, and that the truth had set them, as well as him, free from the past.

While the shadowy cloud lingered like a blessing, Nathan understood that this moment with Monroe, here on Persimmon Hill, had been God's plan all along.

* * * * *

*Look for more books from New York Times
bestselling author Linda Goodnight
later this year!*

*And to read previous titles from
Linda Goodnight, look for:*

To Protect His Children
Keeping Them Safe
The Cowboy's Journey Home
Her Secret Son

*Available now wherever
Love Inspired books are sold!*

Get 4 FREE REWARDS!

We'll send you 2 FREE Books plus 2 FREE Mystery Gifts.

FREE
Value Over
$20

Both the **Harlequin® Special Edition** and **Harlequin® Heartwarming™** series feature compelling novels filled with stories of love and strength where the bonds of friendship, family and community unite.

YES! Please send me 2 FREE novels from the Harlequin Special Edition or Harlequin Heartwarming series and my 2 FREE gifts (gifts are worth about $10 retail). After receiving them, if I don't wish to receive any more books, I can return the shipping statement marked "cancel." If I don't cancel, I will receive 6 brand-new Harlequin Special Edition books every month and be billed just $5.49 each in the U.S. or $6.24 each in Canada, a savings of at least 12% off the cover price, or 4 brand-new Harlequin Heartwarming Larger-Print books every month and be billed just $6.24 each in the U.S. or $6.74 each in Canada, a savings of at least 19% off the cover price. It's quite a bargain! Shipping and handling is just 50¢ per book in the U.S. and $1.25 per book in Canada.* I understand that accepting the 2 free books and gifts places me under no obligation to buy anything. I can always return a shipment and cancel at any time by calling the number below. The free books and gifts are mine to keep no matter what I decide.

Choose one: ☐ **Harlequin Special Edition**   ☐ **Harlequin Heartwarming**
(235/335 HDN GRJV)   **Larger-Print**
(161/361 HDN GRJV)

Name (please print)

Address   Apt. #

City   State/Province   Zip/Postal Code

Email: Please check this box ☐ if you would like to receive newsletters and promotional emails from Harlequin Enterprises ULC and its affiliates. You can unsubscribe anytime.

Mail to the **Harlequin Reader Service:**
IN U.S.A.: P.O. Box 1341, Buffalo, NY 14240-8531
IN CANADA: P.O. Box 603, Fort Erie, Ontario L2A 5X3

Want to try 2 free books from another series! Call 1-800-873-8635 or visit www.ReaderService.com.

*Terms and prices subject to change without notice. Prices do not include sales taxes, which will be charged (if applicable) based on your state or country of residence. Canadian residents will be charged applicable taxes. Offer not valid in Quebec. This offer is limited to one order per household. Books received may not be as shown. Not valid for current subscribers to the Harlequin Special Edition or Harlequin Heartwarming series. All orders subject to approval. Credit or debit balances in a customer's account(s) may be offset by any other outstanding balance owed by or to the customer. Please allow 4 to 6 weeks for delivery. Offer available while quantities last.

Your Privacy—Your information is being collected by Harlequin Enterprises ULC, operating as Harlequin Reader Service. For a complete summary of the information we collect, how we use this information and to whom it is disclosed, please visit our privacy notice located at corporate.harlequin.com/privacy-notice. From time to time we may make your personal information with reputable third parties. If you wish to opt out of this sharing of your personal information, please visit readerservice.com/consumerschoice or call 1-800-873-8635. **Notice to California Residents**—Under California law, you have specific rights to control and access your data. For more information on these rights and how to exercise them, visit corporate.harlequin.com/california-privacy.

HSEHW22R3

COMING NEXT MONTH FROM
Love Inspired

HIS FORGOTTEN AMISH LOVE
by Rebecca Kertz
Two years ago, David Troyer asked to court Fannie Miller...then disappeared without a trace. Suddenly he's back with no memory of her, and she's tasked with catering his family reunion. Where has he been and why has he forgotten her? Will her heart be broken all over again?

THE AMISH SPINSTER'S DILEMMA
by Jocelyn McClay
When a mysterious *Englisch* granddaughter is dropped into widower Thomas Reihl's life, he turns to neighbor Emma Beiler for help. The lonely spinster bonds with the young girl and helps Thomas teach her their Amish ways. Can they both convince Thomas that he needs to start living—and loving—again?

A FRIEND TO TRUST
K-9 Companions • by Lee Tobin McClain
Working at a summer camp isn't easy for Pastor Nate Fisher. Especially since he's sharing the director job with standoffish Hayley Harris. But when Nate learns a secret about one of their campers that affects Hayley, he'll have to decide if their growing connection can withstand the truth.

THE COWBOY'S LITTLE SECRET
Wyoming Ranchers • by Jill Kemerer
Struggling cattle rancher Austin Watkins can't believe his son's nanny is quitting. Cassie Berber wants to pursue her dreams in the big city—even though she cares for the infant and his dad. Can Austin convince her to stay and build a home with them in Wyoming?

LOVING THE RANCHER'S CHILDREN
Hope Crossing • by Mindy Obenhaus
Widower Jake Walker needs a nanny for his kids. But with limited options in their small town, he turns to former friend Alli Krenek. Alli doesn't want anything to do with the single dad, but when she finds herself falling for his children, she'll try to overcome their past and see what the future holds...

HIS SWEET SURPRISE
by Angie Dicken
Returning to his family's orchard, Lance Hudson is seeking a fresh start. He never expects to be working alongside his first love, single mom Piper Gray. When Piper reveals she's the mother of a child he never knew about, Lance must decide if he'll step up and be the man she needs.

LOOK FOR THESE AND OTHER LOVE INSPIRED BOOKS WHEREVER BOOKS ARE SOLD, INCLUDING MOST BOOKSTORES, SUPERMARKETS, DISCOUNT STORES AND DRUGSTORES.

LICNM0423

HARLEQUIN
PLUS

Try the best multimedia subscription service for romance readers like you!

Read, Watch and Play.

Experience the easiest way to get the romance content you crave.

Start your **FREE TRIAL** at
<u>www.harlequinplus.com/freetrial</u>.